Max took her hand and raised it to his lips, placed a delicate kiss on her palm. "Good night, Lily."

Dear Reader,

Lily has two dreams, and now that finding love has proved to be a problem, she's looking for the other one—a baby.

When Max comes back into her life, he's the last man she'd ever consider for either dream, but life has a funny way of throwing caution to the wind.

Max has had a difficult few years and he's no intention of getting caught up in love and possibly hurting anyone.

Sparks are flying between the two of them from the get-go. Can they deal with their rocky past and let go their hang-ups to find love?

I hope you enjoy reading their story and finding out how they get over the hurdles facing them.

All the best,

Sue MacKay

THE GP'S SECRET
BABY WISH

———

SUE MacKAY

HARLEQUIN

**MEDICAL
ROMANCE**

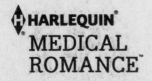

HARLEQUIN®
MEDICAL ROMANCE™

Recycling programs
for this product may
not exist in your area.

ISBN-13: 978-1-335-40425-1

The GP's Secret Baby Wish

Harlequin Enterprises ULC
22 Adelaide St. West, 40th Floor
Toronto, Ontario M5H 4E3, Canada
www.Harlequin.com

Printed in U.S.A.

Sue MacKay lives with her husband in New Zealand's beautiful Marlborough Sounds, with the water on her doorstep and the birds and the trees at her back door. It is the perfect setting to indulge her passions of entertaining friends by cooking them sumptuous meals, drinking fabulous wine, going for hill walks or kayaking around the bay—and, of course, writing stories.

Books by Sue MacKay

Harlequin Medical Romance

London Hospital Midwives
A Fling to Steal Her Heart

SOS Docs
Redeeming Her Brooding Surgeon

Baby Miracle in the ER
Surprise Twins for the Surgeon
ER Doc's Forever Gift
The Italian Surgeon's Secret Baby
Take a Chance on the Single Dad
The Nurse's Twin Surprise
Reclaiming Her Army Doc Husband
The Nurse's Secret

Visit the Author Profile page
at Harlequin.com for more titles.

Dedicated to Lindsay, my rock.

PROLOGUE

Run, Lily. Now. Get away from Max Bryant. Now. Before it's too late. Before your heart's inextricably caught up in his charm...

Her pulse was racing, while at the same time her body warmed to him, and confusion reigned in her head. Max was a playboy who thought women were there for one thing only, namely keeping him happy, and here she was in his bed. She'd used him for her own gain. Except now she wanted more of him. Friendship, sharing and caring. Maybe even a *future*? That wasn't going to happen. He wasn't the settle down kind of guy and she'd already experienced a relationship where her partner had broken all those promises.

Lily shuddered. Just the idea of climbing out of Max's bed for the last time felt as though chains were holding her back from escaping the growing sense that he was getting under her skin and waking her up in ways that wouldn't, or couldn't, work with him. Not long term, and that was the only way ahead for her.

They'd had a spectacular few days, but she had to remember how he gave her grief about being wealthy, almost as though that was more important than anything else about her, like he didn't see her for who she was, so she had to move away, move on. Anyway, it was too soon after Aaron had broken her heart by blatantly cheating.

Short, rapid breaths escaped Lily's mouth. Her throat hurt from trying not to yell her frustration at not just finding Max likable but that he'd shown her a softer side than he ever showed at work. This wasn't meant to have happened. It was supposed to be a fling with no feelings involved, merely a way of boosting her ego and proving to herself that men did find her attractive. That Aaron was wrong to have called her uptight and dull—his excuse for having sex with other women in their bed. She'd needed to gain back some control over relationships, short or long, to fix her heart.

Max was sprawled beside her, legs spread wide and one hand behind his head and one on her thigh as he slept the sleep of the dead after the most amazing sex she'd ever experienced. Apart from the sex they'd shared over the previous two days, that was. 'Shared' being the remarkable feature. Full credit to the man. He gave as much as he took, which probably explained his popularity with the females from work he spent extracurricular time with. She hadn't felt uptight with him, or dull if the sounds emitting from his generous, exciting mouth when she'd ridden him were an indicator.

It would be too easy to roll on top of that muscular body and tease him awake. Lust was pulling at her, heating up fast. Lily began turning towards him. Stopped. No. She mustn't. She wasn't ready to trust another man.

She didn't usually go for casual sex, but with Aaron's words ringing in her ears once too often she'd taken up Max's invitation to join him in bed three days ago after a particularly hectic, adrenalin-fuelled night on duty in the emergency department, despite him being a lady's man with a belt full of notches.

Or was it because of that she'd done this? To show she was just as desirable as those other women? Not that Aaron would notice, and if he did, it was too late. She mightn't be over his hurtful words or the image of what he'd been doing with that nurse in their shower, but she was over him.

Lily began sliding towards the edge of the bed. She needed to get out of there while she had the strength to go. It was one thing to have beyond amazing sex with Max, quite another to think there'd be anything more. His reputation for loving and leaving went before him, and she didn't intend to become a statistic. Better to exit, head high, in control, even if behind her ribs there was a rough pattering going on.

You're on the rebound.

Relief assailed her. Yes, rebound love. No, don't use the L word about this man. Rebound or not, it wasn't love keeping her awake long after he'd rolled off her. Whatever the hell it was, she wasn't waiting around to find out. She was done and dusted with their fling. They'd continue working together and forget all about these few days. It seemed easy, yet doubt fluttered through her mind.

Max's hand tightened, loosened on her thigh.

Squashing that doubt, she waited until his breathing returned to normal. If only her lungs would do the same. Impossible with the heat that hand caused to fill her empty heart. Why should she sneak away? She'd see him at work in five hours. She might as well be open and honest. Lily stood up and snatched up her clothes from the floor, started shoving herself into them.

'Where're you off to?'

So much for thinking he was out for the

count. 'Home.' The zip on her jeans caught in the fabric.

'Come back to bed. We've got a few hours left before we have to be on duty.'

'No, Max.' The zip wouldn't budge. Giving up, she tugged her jersey over her head and down below her waist.

The sound of his body sliding up the bed told her he was wide awake. There was a wicked glint in his eyes, reminding her of all he promised her body, which didn't help her determination to get out of there. 'Sure I can't tempt you?'

He could do that, all right. Only he had to get out from under her skin. 'Sorry, but I'm away now.' Tying up the laces of her shoes, she said, 'It's been great, but I'm done.'

His head jerked higher. 'You think?'

'I know.' Slinging her bag over her shoulder, she headed to the door. 'See you tonight. On duty,' she added, to make sure he was understanding her intent.

He was off the bed and standing between her and the door so quickly she gulped. 'Not so fast.'

It was hard to remember why she was in a hurry to leave when she took in the sight before her. Tall, lean, muscular without being too hard, every inch of his body was to die for. Her mouth dried. What was she doing, walking away?

'Why, Lily? And don't tell me you haven't had a blast these past few days.'

'I have. That's what it was all about. Now it's time to move on.' She couldn't look him in the eye. He might see her hesitancy, might recognise he disturbed her on a level she wasn't prepared for, didn't want.

'Move on to what? Another fling?'

Now she did fix her eyes on his face. 'You have a problem with that? With your reputation?' Did he have to be so good looking?

'Yes, I do.'

Got it. 'You can't handle the fact I'm leaving first. I'm supposed to cling to you and beg you to let me stay, not get out of bed and go.'

'Get off your high horse, Lily. I've enjoyed the time we've had together here and thought there was more to come. Seems I was wrong. Should've known you'd exercise your control even over something like this.'

'My control?' she blustered. But he was right in one respect. She was trying to stay in control of herself, but not of him. He could go and do whatever he liked as long as she got him out from under her skin.

'You have everything in hand, never face difficulties.'

He hadn't heard how the surgeon had treated her when the story had been rife on the hospital grapevine? Of course, it'd happened weeks before Max had started working in ED. It probably didn't qualify as a difficulty to this man, who thought relationships were all about sex and not getting involved. 'I'd have thought you'd be thankful I'm going and not hanging on for every look you might send my way.' Another light-bulb moment struck. 'You're not used to being ditched.'

The exaggerated eye roll he did told her she'd hit the nail on the head even before he drawled, 'Naturally.'

Damn, he was full of himself. But she'd known that and had still slept with him for her own needs. She'd had a great time, too. Too great, if that niggling sense of losing control was anything to go by. 'Get over yourself, Max. I've seen the other women you've hurt but I will not be treated like something you've used and tossed aside. I came into this with my eyes wide and knowing it was going to be short-lived. I will not be going around with tears in my eyes and hoping that you'll give me a second chance. Because I don't feel that.'

She swept his body with her gaze, taking in the sight one more time, pretending he was easy to walk away from, and that she hadn't lied, ignoring the thumping of her heart. Stepping around him before she did something stupid like run her finger down his sternum, she muttered, 'See you later.' Hopefully it would be as manic as Thursday and Friday nights had always been so there'd been no time for small talk, or coffee, or drinking in the sight of Max's tight butt in his blue scrubs whenever he bent over a bed to check out a patient.

Tonight was the beginning of the rest of the time they worked together. She just had to remember she was desirable whenever he looked at her with that disbelief blinking at her now. If she wasn't, the sex wouldn't have been so intense and hot, and touching. Max hadn't been making that up. She paused. 'Thank you.'

He turned his back on her.

CHAPTER ONE

LILY SHRANK DEEPER into her warm jacket as the bus pulled away, and stared up the wide pathway leading to the massive building housing Auckland's Remuera Medical Hub. 'What *am* I doing?'

Preparing to start her dream job was all very well, but working with Max Bryant again had her head banging with doubts. Could she make it work, or would they combust the moment they set eyes on each other and make life awkward at the very least? She shivered—but not from the cold. It was a risk but one she'd decided to take in order to have this job. Max had never quite left her, occasionally popping into her mind to remind her how she'd walked away from what might possibly have been something amazing. But she had, and had found love with another man, or so she'd thought. She'd got that wrong as well.

Shouting broke through her hesitation and

seemed to be coming from beyond the bus, which was moving on.

'Lily Scott,' a male called. 'Lily, over here.'

Her heart thumped once. Max? Yes. Her mouth dried. Of course it would be. Straight into the fire without time to breathe. She looked around, saw the man waving from further along the busy road. Another, harder, thump. So much for being prepared for this.

Three years and lots of living had passed and amongst all that Max had occasionally sneaked under her skin, reminding her of what they'd shared briefly, of what she'd walked away from because she hadn't trusted him not to hurt her when she'd been vulnerable. Because she hadn't trusted her own strength to remain immune to him.

'One of my patients has fallen. I might need a hand,' he called.

'Coming.' Lily's fingers tingled as she stared at Max while weaving through the rush-hour traffic. He'd caused her to think twice about accepting the position here. She'd thought twice and had taken it anyway because their history was exactly that. History. Yet just hearing his voice brought an image of him calling out to her from his bed, telling her to get under the sheets quick fast. He'd been funny and generous, unlike the ego she'd worked with.

She did regret the awkward way they'd finished their fling. They could have found a way to get along comfortably if nothing else, but instead the barriers she'd raised between them once she'd understood how easily she lost control around him had turned him against her. For the next two long months they had continued working as junior doctors in the emergency department, barely communicating unless it had been about patients.

Someone bumping into her sent her tripping a few steps before she straightened up and blindly pushed through the crowd to the kerb, taking elbows and knocks in her stride, concentrating on getting across the road.

A young woman lay sprawled on the pavement, her left ankle at an odd angle and her hand gripping her left wrist. Kneeling beside her was Max.

Lily gulped, looked at the woman then back at Max. His once straight black hair had become wavy with bright streaks of grey. Lines accentuated the forthright chin and sharpened once soft, come-hither eyes. He no longer looked quite like the man who'd had more notches than leather on his belt. The man she'd slept with three years ago between relationship disasters to boost her confidence. He'd aged. A lot more than to be expected in the time since she'd last seen him, surely? Had something terrible happened? She swallowed the urge to ask and squatted opposite him to focus on the woman cursing ferociously between them and not on him.

'Michelle, what happened?' Max asked, with barely a glance in Lily's direction.

'Some doped-up ass charged off the bus I was getting on,' the woman ground out through the pain contorting her narrow face. 'He shoved me so hard I landed on my wrist and leg on the concrete.'

Lily sucked in a breath through clenched teeth. She couldn't ignore him or he'd think nothing had changed with her. And it had. Another man walking out on her had taught her to be stronger than ever and look out for herself and her own needs, which included getting onside with this man.

'Hello, Max.' Her tongue was in a knot, belying her resolve to be sensible about him, to work alongside him without rehashing the past. The sizzle that had led to three hot, unforgettable nights was taunting her. She'd walked away from those bewitching sensations with her head high, heart unsteady, and the sensible side of her brain telling her to get out while it was still possible. After all the years in between, Max had her in a pickle within moments? Her hand tightened convulsively.

'Hi, Lily.' His nod was brief, his glance even shorter. 'Not a great way to start a new job, meeting your first patient out here in the cold.'

'She's going to be my patient?'

'Yes, while I'm her sports doctor. Twenty minutes ago she bounced out of my office on her way to catch the bus to training.' He was gently touching Michelle's swollen ankle above her running shoe.

'Yeah, and now look at me,' the woman snapped.

Lily focused on their patient, not on Max and how different he looked and sounded. He seemed more serious, with less ego on display. 'Let me look at your wrist.' Like her ankle, it was already swelling. 'Can you bend it at all?'

Michelle complied by trying to bend it up and down. 'Afraid not.' Neither could she move it sideways. 'You going to take my shoe off, Max?'

He shook his head. 'No, it's best to leave it on to hold everything in place. If there's a fracture I don't want the bones moving.'

That deep, sexy voice brought back memories best forgotten. When accepting the position at one of the city's most reputable medical centres, she'd determined to be friendly towards him while keeping her distance, had hoped to feel only indifference, not have her blood racing and her toes tingling from only a glance. Gulp. When it came to medicine and learning all there was to know, he'd been excellent during his internship and that was all that mattered here, not the brief fling that had led to disappointment in herself for *feeling* something for him. Making a success of this job included getting on with Max.

'How's that wrist, Lily?' he asked, finally looking straight at her for a moment.

'There's little movement because of the swelling. Michelle, how painful is it? One to ten, ten highest.'

'Eight. Ankle's ten.' Despair began pouring out of Michelle's mouth. 'That creep's ruined everything I've worked so hard for. Where is he? He pushed me and now he's run away. The coward.'

Shaking her head to refocus and put aside the flare of interest Max's look had created, Lily reached for Michelle's wrist again. 'I want to check further.' With one finger, she began gently pressing the joints.

'It hurts like hell. I reckon it's broken. And my ankle. How am I going to play with the netball team in England now? Tell me that.'

'We don't know anything for certain.' Max was again gently feeling the tissue above the shoe but quickly stopped when Michelle groaned. 'You need X-rays.'

'Why bother? I felt the ankle crack. The pain's excruciating. I won't be able to train for months. So much for all the hard work I've put in. It's come to nothing because of some idiot who doesn't have the gumption to stay and see if he can do anything to help me.' Tears spewed down Michelle's white face. 'Where is he?' she yelled.

'Take it easy. You're in good physical condition, which is a bonus.' From what little Lily could see, Michelle must work out a lot. 'Let's find out what the damage is first,' she said, her heart squeezing for the woman who was obviously a very fit athlete. There was no denying that she probably wouldn't be playing netball any time soon, though. 'I'm sure Max has ideas on how to get you up and about as fast as possible once we know.'

His head shot up and he stared at her for a moment then replied, 'You bet.' He looked to Michelle and smiled encouragingly.

Lily fought her disappointment. No smile for her. This wasn't how meeting up with Max again for the first time was meant to feel. Awkward, not direct and simple. Not that she'd been silly enough to think it would be quite that easy. But she was home for good and wanted the best out of this career opportunity. As for men, she was done with them. Except for one purpose and that would take a lot of careful thought and good judgement before it came about.

Since becoming single again, a slow, quiet tick-tock had begun deep inside where her heart lay, saying that time was rushing by, that she might never find a man to love her for who she was and to give her the family she longed for. A man who was kind, sensible, generous of spirit and downright decent.

Not Max, then.

She shivered. There was no chance of that with his ego and way of using charm to get everything he wanted. He'd also shown a lack of concern for the women whose hearts he'd broken. Intelligent and clever, he could also be self-centred and egotistical.

He was talking to Michelle, calm and direct. 'You want me to ring your mother and let her know what's happened once we've got you on your way?'

'I guess.' Michelle scrubbed at her face with her uninjured hand, blinking rapidly.

Scrabbling in her bag, Lily found a pocket pack of tissues. 'Here you go.'

'Thanks.'

Max continued talking as though nothing out of the ordinary was happening. 'You need to focus on getting treatment and arranging physio as soon as it's feasible. As I said, you're strong and fit. Those things are on your side in this and will help you back to normal sooner than most people.'

Lily kept watching Michelle while listening to the determination for his patient in Max's voice. It was his way of saying she couldn't fail now. Kindness hidden behind his medical analysis, and that surprised her. If she were ever to consider a man as a father for her child, he would have to be kind.

Just then Max glanced her way, a brief wry smile on those full lips. And something jolted deep inside her. Something warm, and tight with apprehension. It couldn't be. Let's face it. When he'd smiled at her on the final morning she'd woken up in his bed, there'd been no jolting going on. Or so she'd told herself. It had been more remorse for joining Max's statistics and fear she'd let him get to her.

Let it go. Falling for that smile now was not on her agenda. Starting at the medical hub was all about being a doctor and getting on with plans for the future, it had nothing to do with him. But it was impossible to ignore the fluttering in her belly. Soft and continual, as though she was being told to look at Max in a whole new way. It was becoming more obvious every minute how much he'd changed. Concern for his patient was normal, but not the self-deprecating humour he'd briefly shown her. She tightened her stomach to quieten the flutter.

Max had always worked hard and sucked up knowledge like a sponge. That wouldn't have changed. It'd been important for him to do well in his career, which had resonated with her own ambitions, and the only aspect she knew about him that wasn't full of his ego. He'd always accepted when he was wrong if it meant learning something to improve his skills. His patients would no doubt like him a lot.

Something clicked in her brain, solving a pesky riddle that had been hovering in the background since her interview with the partners of the centre. When she'd known him previously Max had been fervent about specialising in surgery.

'Sports doctor?' And GP. What *had* happened in the intervening years?

He told her with a guarded look, 'There's a wheelchair in the room behind Reception. Would you mind getting it?'

'No problem.' Had he deliberately avoided her question? Or was he merely reminding her they were with a patient?

'Door on the left. Avoid Reception and everyone or we'll be waiting out here for ages.'

Where the function she'd been heading to, before Max had called out, was being held. 'On it. What about an ambulance?'

'I'll call when we're inside, out of the cold,' Max replied.

Within minutes she'd returned to the scene with a nifty wheelchair, and locked the brakes in preparation to loading Michelle. 'Here we go.'

Max straightened up. 'Between us we'll lift you onto the chair, Michelle.'

Michelle had other ideas. 'Take a side each and pull me up. I can stand on my good leg.'

'Fine.' Max obviously knew not to argue. She was quickly in the chair and Max was rolling her up the incline to the side door of the medical centre.

Inside, Lily followed them down the hall to an office that the diplomas on the wall told her was Max's. Again, she wanted to ask about his change in direction but managed to swallow the question. He was affecting her with his focused approach, which was nothing like the vibrant, the-world-is-my-oyster guy she'd known. This quieter, still smiling but in a softer way, man was knocking her long-held beliefs that he was all about himself.

Max held a hand out to her. 'Welcome aboard, Lily.'

She stared at that hand, her skin warming with memories.

'Lily?' He was retracting his welcome gesture.

Quickly sliding her hand into his large one, she gave it a shake. 'Thanks, Max. I'm excited about working here.' *About seeing you.* Jerking free, she stepped back, glancing across to confused eyes. 'I mean it,' she added. *I think.*

'Good.' He turned to the other woman. 'Michelle, Lily Scott's taking over from Sarah in a couple of weeks so technically she's going to be your GP. Lily, Michelle Baxter.'

Lily reached for her hand and shook it. 'Wish I'd met you in better circumstances.'

'So do I.' Michelle's cheeks flushed. 'Sorry, ignore me. I'm acting like a spoilt brat, but it's truly frustrating.'

'You're fine. Anyone would be furious at what's occurred.' But bad things happened to people. There was no avoiding them. She knew that all too well.

Only six months ago she'd arrived home at the Singapore apartment she'd shared with her fiancé, Leo, to find him waiting, bags packed, while a one-way ticket to Scotland and his passport had lain on the table. He was heading back to his home town and she wasn't invited. He'd decided to go back to the girlfriend he'd broken up with only months before meeting Lily. A woman Lily had never heard of until that day. Apparently Leo had been in constant contact with her for months and the lure of what they'd once had was too strong to ignore. Stronger than his feelings for Lily. She'd loved him and it hadn't counted.

Two broken relationships showed how unlucky she was in love, had proved how unlovable she must be. Two men had cheated on her. There were only so many heartbreaks she could survive, and Max wasn't causing her another. After their fling he'd been cool towards her, suggesting he might've actually been glad she'd stopped it, and that had added to her sense that she was unlovable when it came to finding a soul mate. She'd better remember that. It was a strong reason for contemplating having a baby on her own.

Lily had been as much furious at being duped by Leo as she had felt hurt. He hadn't wanted children, something he'd failed to mention until he'd been leaving. That dishonesty had been a bitter pill to swallow, but over the intervening months it had been dissolving and now she was almost relieved that relationship was over, as though Leo hadn't been as much the love of her life as she'd believed.

Second best because going for the real thing

was too risky, hurt too much when it failed. She just wasn't good at relationships. Men might let her down, go to other women for comfort, but she'd be a loving, devoted mother. No one would take that away from her.

Family meant everything to her, and if she had to have her own baby in a different way then so be it. No more hoping for love to come her way, or having her own thrown back in her face. She'd selflessly love her child alongside her parents, brothers and sisters-in-law. As her mouth curved upward, her heart slowed. A baby. Her baby. Wow. If she got past the idea of a stranger fathering her infant, it would be amazing.

Max was talking to Michelle. 'Between the three of us, we'll get you back on your feet and beating the hell out of those Poms.'

'You think?' Hope flicked on in their patient's eyes. 'You'd better be right.' The hope disappeared as fast as it had arrived.

Gathering her scattered thoughts, Lily added her bit to Max's encouragement. 'We'll do better than that.' Again an unfamiliar warmth touched Lily's skin. Max had included her in the scenario with Michelle when he could have claimed it was a sports injury and therefore his case. She hadn't expected that. She hugged herself. People did change. She had. She'd faced her demons and found a way to move forward.

'It won't be a walk in the park, but we'll make it happen. You've got to stay positive. That's as important as the rest.' Max locked a formidable gaze on their patient. 'I'll get you some pain relief and phone for an ambulance.'

Michelle nodded. 'The sooner the better for both.'

Through the partially open door laughter reached them. Max glanced over. 'You'd better get in there and start meeting everyone, Lily. I'll look after Michelle and join the fray when she's on her way.'

She couldn't believe the disappointment making itself known in her head at his suggestion. Disappointed she wasn't spending more time with Max? She wasn't admitting that so it must be to do with getting to know her first patient. 'It's Sarah's farewell night. I'll stay with Michelle while you phone for the ambulance.'

'Get on with you. Everyone's wanting to welcome you to the centre. I'm going to stay here until Michelle's on her way.' He held the phone up. 'I've got painkillers in my bag.'

There was no arguing with him. She gave in on a sigh. 'I guess I'd better put in an appearance before they think I'm a no show.'

'You might want to check your face in the

mirror,' Max nodded to a cupboard door on the far wall. 'You've got a smear on your cheek.'

She blinked. 'Thanks.'

He grinned. 'No problem.'

Showing her care and understanding was new. Nothing like the guy who'd basically called her a control freak when she'd turned him down after three hot nights together.

Tonight he was presenting an image she'd not seen before. Or had she been so determined to find fault with him to protect herself that she'd missed what had been right before her eyes? He'd tweaked her curiosity with his gentleness in bed, and the heat between them had been a conflagration. He certainly hadn't appeared to find her lacking as a sexual partner, but she hadn't hung around long enough to risk that wearing off and having that sense of something wonderful happening between them expanding to the point she'd be devastated when he moved on. Because he would have without a doubt. It had been his way.

Yet now she wanted to find out more. The unknown made life tricky, increased the possibility of something going wrong. Failure was something she rarely experienced, except with lovers. Growing up with two brothers who had continually goaded her into proving she was as good as them at any job on the farm had been a constant battle, but she'd always taken up the challenges. Her brothers had helped her grow a backbone and become resilient, but they had never taught her to protect her heart, hence she gave it away too easily. Not any more, though, except to her baby when he or she came about.

Ducking into the bathroom, Lily wiped the smudge of mascara from under her eye and laughed at herself for getting excited over Max. He might look and sound different, but Max was Max, end of story. Best keep that in the forefront of her mind. She'd returned home to get on with being a doctor in a fabulous centre. Starting now, she would not let bygone hurts distract her, would put them behind her and be open to opportunities as they arose.

'There you are.' Devlin, one of the partners, approached her with a welcoming smile when she entered the reception area. 'Thought I'd have to send out a search party.'

'A patient had an accident getting on the bus. Max's getting her sorted now.' She resisted the urge to hug Devlin in case anyone got the wrong idea. He was her father's lifelong friend, having grown up on a neighbouring farm, though Devlin had left to become a doctor while her father had remained on the land. She and Devlin had agreed to be open about knowing each other well, but wouldn't flaunt it. She was here on her own merits, not because of family contacts. 'Being here is great.' Even with Max in the picture.

Max stood in the doorway, shoulder against the frame, watching Lily doing the circuit, his hand still tingling from where her palm had touched his. Shock had flicked in and out of her eyes, a similar shock to the one that had torpedoed his gut. The same sensation he'd known with her three years ago. Apparently not even the gruelling episode he'd suffered since then had fixed that. Being totally at ease with everyone came naturally to her but, then, coming from a wealthy background would boost anyone's confidence, and Lily had an abundance of that.

When they'd worked together in ED, she'd twice appeared on television at her father's side for the national wine awards, dressed in stunning dresses and standing confidently on dangerously high heels, smiling as though she'd won and not her parent. It was something he'd given her a hard time about, and now regretted. There were a few things to do with Lily he regretted, one being how their fling had finished so abruptly. He hadn't taken it well, had been rude to her to hide his hurt. Unbelievably he'd begun to see her as a woman who mattered, who he just might be able to take a chance with.

Lily had been special in bed, generous while not trying to impress, unlike the Lily he'd thought he knew, and unlike other women he'd slept with. Her enthusiasm for life and wanting to share that with him during that short time had touched him in a way he'd not known before. It had been something he'd wanted to explore, to share and give back, which he never did with the women he dated. Yet there'd been a red flag warning him about finding more to her than he could cope with, and failing to let go of her when the fling ran its course.

It had been something he'd wanted to explore, yet had been wary of—worried he might find more to her than he could cope with. A reason for remaining single until he qualified was the oath he'd sworn to himself to avoid getting sidetracked and maybe failing. He'd had to show his father he was worthy of him, that when his mother had left them, taking his sister with her, it hadn't meant he wasn't lovable. The problem with that was that his father didn't do loving and caring, more like demanding and tough. It was only recently that he had realised that for Dad that was being loving.

His eyes were still tracking Lily. She was gorgeous with a capital G.

Michelle was impressed. 'Straightforward

and no promises she mightn't be able to keep,' had been her opinion.

Not that he could fault Michelle's decision to take Lily on as her GP. Lily didn't overwork sympathy or try to impress just for the sake of it. She could put on a show when needed, though never when it came to her medical career. He sighed. She had been dedicated to learning all she could. *Huh?* Max jerked upright. He hadn't thought of it before, but he could see it now. That hadn't been about making herself look good. Lily soaking up knowledge and then using it with patients carefully and confidently but quietly, not showing off to anyone. He'd seen her in action and not credited her with what it was worth, too busy following his own path, busy living life to the full, working all hours, and not being impressed when anyone had got in the way or turned him down. He had never stopped to see people for who they were.

Except that time that Lily had said no to another night together. Then he had paused, looking for the Lily others saw. He'd felt a heel as the beautiful, caring woman came to light under his scrutiny. She'd been popular with everyone in the ED and he'd not noticed that before. After their fling, he'd felt there was something more to her that he couldn't quite grasp.

Something that lit a fire in his belly. Something he was afraid to confront in case it got to him in unexpected ways, so he'd quickly moved on to other more willing opportunities. But he'd never forgotten those nights, never accepted she'd pulled the plug on him. It had stung. He'd wanted more and she hadn't.

She'd woken him up to the fact that he had usually been the one walking away, and hadn't been kind in the way he'd gone about it. It was scary how quickly she'd got under his skin when they had become intimate. For the first time ever he'd begun considering other possibilities, such as a real, loving, permanent relationship.

That had made him consider the women he'd bedded and how his love 'em and leave 'em attitude might have hurt them. He hadn't stopped bedding women, but he had become more considerate of their feelings and worked hard at not hurting them by explaining straight up that he wasn't looking for a permanent relationship.

Taking a long, deep breath, he studied the female who'd had his teeth grinding from the moment he'd learned she was joining Remuera Medical Hub. Sparks were flickering in his gut. Her shoulder-length copper-coloured hair gleamed as it always had.

Her one vanity, he'd once heard her say to a nurse and had spluttered into his water bottle, thinking she was nothing but vanity with her stylish hair, perfectly manicured nails, elegant shoes that must've hurt like hell on a hectic day in the department. That hadn't stopped him taking her to bed, though. Hell, he really hadn't been the nice guy he'd thought he was.

Financially he'd struggled through med school and her attitude had rubbed him up the wrong way. Only once again he'd been wrong. She hadn't pushed people's faces in her good fortune, and really, looking back, she had only been herself, a well-dressed, kind woman who had wanted to help people as much as he did.

Her tall, slim figure had filled out a little now, giving her a more curvaceous shape that suited her—and tightened him uncomfortably. The elegantly simple navy trousers and jacket with a cream blouse added to her appeal. A straightforward, this-is-who-I-am look that had him wanting to get behind it and learn more about why she got him in a tangle. Her face had matured into a beautiful woman's countenance. Why had he sulked when she'd walked away from his bed? Turning him down with no explanation wasn't an excuse to be rude. Quite the opposite. Lily had been the catalyst for him to start putting others before himself.

She turned from talking to Devlin and caught his eye. Her smile slipped then returned; not false as he used to expect but genuine. Now, there was a first, and one he should grab with both hands—if he wasn't adamant about not getting into a relationship. There was no changing his mind now.

The past few years had taught him to make the most of life and the people he met, not to wreck any chances for happiness by being full of himself. Apart from surviving, it was the best to come out of his battle with cancer, and one he held onto tight. It had helped him get through the ghastly, dark days of surgery and chemo, and a new, edgy treatment. It had kept him grounded in unexpected ways—appreciating the honest kindness of the nurses and doctors who had treated him, learning the other side of a medical problem from that of the doctor's perspective, finding he had still been breathing every morning when he'd first opened his eyes to another day of hell.

Oh, yes, it had been a steep learning curve that had taught him things about himself he'd never suspected. He was worthy of giving and accepting love, and giving was way better than taking.

He'd also learned the future came with no guarantees. Hence the reason now for never marrying or having children. It would be selfish to ask a woman to share his uncertainties. Looking at Lily, it made him sad. Not because they now had a chance of getting on like they never had, but because, with her ease and laughter, and love of life and people, she reminded him of those things he did want and had promised himself not to look for in case he caused more pain.

His mother and sister leaving had broken him, and filled him with a belief that women would never give him their hearts completely. Somehow those nights with Lily and the way she had left had made him sit up and take a long hard look at himself and why he'd treated women indifferently. Not any more. Now the rare times he was intimate he hoped he was kind and caring, and made no promises for the future. The past couldn't be undone, but he'd learned and changed, hopefully for the better.

Lily was coming his way. Hell, she'd had him smiling at her with genuine care when they'd been dealing with Michelle's accident. He'd kept his smiles for his patient, though, wary of letting Lily sense he was comfortable and happy to be with her. Their old one-upmanship hadn't resurfaced yet, and hopefully wouldn't. She'd been friendly, at ease in a way he hadn't known with any woman. He liked that. His teeth had finally stopped grinding. He didn't want her even suspecting he'd had a tough time since they'd last seen each other, so, shoving all thoughts of the past and what might be if he had the guts to take risks down deep where no one would see them, he stepped forward, a light smile lifting his mouth. A genuine smile. For Lily. *Careful.* They had to work together. He had to remain neutral around her. The smile slipped.

'Max, shall we start again? How are you?'

'No need to start over.' They'd done well already. But he hadn't changed so much he'd couldn't resist teasing, because that'd keep her a little further away. 'Hello, Lady Lily. How are you?'

She stared at him for a moment, then knock him down if she didn't burst out laughing. 'Probably in better condition than your over-notched belt used to be. You doing okay?'

Ouch. Suppressing a grimace, he took the hand she held out, and shook it, taking longer this time until a flare of heat scorched his palm. Of course there was warmth when two people shook hands, unless they were in the middle of a blizzard, and there was no sign of that here. 'I'm good.' Fingers crossed. It was a regular habit now, hopefully keeping the medical voo-doos at bay. And any others. 'We seem to have a knack of getting medical positions at the same place, don't we?'

Lily nodded, not sure where he was headed. She went for neutral. 'I'm looking forward to working alongside you again.' The words tasted false. Then she astonished herself. Was her reaction merely a habit from days gone by? Their aversion for each other had had tense periods but had mostly been a sense of having nothing in common, apart from great fun in bed and that uncanny sense that she had to get away from the attraction those nights had created.

She hadn't liked his easy come, easy go attitude towards women, yet she'd slept with him, had become one of those notches because she'd been desperate to feel attractive and possibly even lovable. It hadn't helped that she'd got in deep quickly. She hadn't understood why she'd gone with him. It had been like an invisible string winding her into Max's web and she'd entered not reluctantly but with a need to gain some self-worth. As if she'd chosen the most difficult man to impress to prove she had triumphed over her failings. Max had been exceptional had and made her feel very attractive. A blush filled her cheeks. She looked away, only to immediately bring her gaze back to him.

Max was staring down at her, a glint she remembered too well in those khaki eyes that said he doubted her sincerity. He spoke in that firm way he'd used with Michelle when she had been more concerned about who'd knocked her off the bus than what he'd been saying. 'Let's not get too carried away, Lily.' It sounded as though he was cautioning them both. Then he gave a small smile, and her caution began to slide. 'It's great to have you on board.' His gaze was steady and clear.

Maybe he meant it. That was something to think about. Again, he struck her as having changed a lot. He'd grown up, and was less jaunty. Although he was just as confident as ever, there were new depths to that confidence and, paradoxically, a few cracks. She was as sure as she had ten toes that something awful had befallen Max. Those eyes held a depth of perception she'd not known previously. A care for others that had nothing to do with what he might want, and no one changed like that over a cup of tea.

Withdrawing her hand from his surprisingly gentle touch a little late, her body pinged as though she'd put her finger into an electric socket. 'Thank you.' They would get on fine, and not just to nod at each other as they passed in the hall. 'I can't wait to get started.' This busy medical hub catered to specialities as well as general practice. She wanted to give it her all, carve out a niche that would go on long into the future and support her and her future child, if and when that happened. *Not now, Lily.* To silence those thoughts, she returned to the topic she'd raised earlier. 'I'm surprised to learn you're a GP, with sports medicine your focus.'

His eyes narrowed.

Quickly she said, 'I'm not having a poke at your choice, Max. I love general practice and understand anyone wanting to be a GP. It's just that you were so determined to become an orthopaedic surgeon.'

An abrupt nod. 'I was, but then I had a change of heart and decided I wanted to see more of my patients than a consultation, followed by a few minutes' talking in Theatre before surgery, a final handshake and goodbye.' His shoulders softened while his focus was entirely on her, making her feel warm and comfortable. Odd. Lovely. Just what she liked in a man. 'Too removed for my liking.'

'I totally agree. Then again, I'm starting over with getting to know patients, so I haven't a lot of experience of following through with families, watching them grow and age and get ill and come out the other end, which is why this is a long-term move.' One that would involve a family of two. Her and a child. No more shocks tipping her off track, no more feeling lost and let down, and in need of a kick up the backside to get up again.

Max's face tightened. 'I hear you worked in Singapore until recently.'

'I worked at an international family medical centre in the city. It's a fascinating country and I enjoyed getting out and about when I wasn't working. As for the street food, it was gorgeous.' She missed that as much as anything.

'What brought you back to Auckland?'

'It was time. I never intended setting up permanently overseas.' After Leo had packed his bags, there had been little reason to stay on. He'd know from what everyone here would have told him about her that she was single. It didn't matter. She wasn't looking for a partner, and Max was not the sort of man she was interested in for the father of her baby.

He may have changed, but she couldn't trust throwing a baby in the mix. It was very possible he'd want to take a part in raising a child that was his, not be content with only donating the DNA. He may treat women in an offhand manner, but there was a fierce determination in those veins to do the right thing that would force him to look out for his kin. 'I missed having my family close enough to see them whenever I want, and to support them when needed.'

'How's your niece? Josie, isn't it?'

He remembered her name after all this time? Incredible. It seemed there was more to Max than she'd ever acknowledged. Apparently he hadn't always been focused on himself. Though thinking back to a frightening time when Josie had rolled her wheelchair over a bank, knocking herself out, and had been flown to their ED, there hadn't been many in the department who hadn't known what had happened and to whom. Still, Max remembering more than just there'd been an accident was something else.

'She's done well. There's no holding her back and she's so strong mentally it can be scary.' She laughed. Then stopped. How strange, talking like this, when they'd never done so in the past. 'In fact, she'll be at the Let's Have Fun camp next week.'

Included in that was the camp she'd established for disabled children with her niece in mind. Josie had been born with spina bifida, and had never ceased to amaze Lily with her tenacity. All kids should have resilience, especially those with tough obstacles to get past. The next intake for disabled kids aged ten to fifteen was all about building resilience to the obstacles life threw their way.

'In Whangaparaoa? You know I'll be there?'

Lily nodded. 'Yes, I do.' Being on the board of the charity organisation running the camp, she knew exactly who signed on to help out every time. 'I heard.' From Devlin, who organised staff rotations. Devlin was her strongest backer, and was always on the lookout for medical people to take a turn helping out. Usually, little serious doctoring was required but it was good to have someone there to discuss aches and pains, and how injuries could be overcome without losing confidence. He understood her need for it not to be known she'd initially funded the whole complex. She had kept that under wraps and only her lawyer—being her best friend—her family and Devlin knew.

If anyone was determined it wouldn't take rocket science to find out she'd created the trust and paid for the land and buildings, but hopefully that would never become public knowledge. She couldn't bear to see her face in the news under a heading like 'Daughter of Wealthy Winemaker Sets Up Trust Fund for Disabled'.

Being asked if it was because of Josie would make her furious and distress her niece. It was bad enough going as her father's support to the wine awards, where her dress got more interest than her father's achievements. Her mother refused to go, not wanting to be talked about for her outfit or hairstyle either. But her dad deserved family backing so she put up with the accompanying nonsense.

'I'm looking forward to it. I've taken the whole week off,' Max was saying.

She didn't encourage anyone to sign up only for a day or two. The kids needed the same people working with them throughout the week, not swapping halfway and getting different ideas on how to manage with their personal problems. 'Hope you're packing your sports gear. You'll be needed to referee and coach as well as deal with sprains and aches.'

Max watched her intently, as though he sensed more behind her words.

She'd got carried away. He'd never been stupid. 'I've gone with Josie before, and I'm on the board.' She knew everything about the camp and what went on, right down to the latest repair job by the plumber for a leaking drain.

'Will you be there next week?'

Damn. Walked into that one. 'I'll be along the road at the family's beach house, available if Josie needs me.' An *aha* light went on in his eyes. 'Naturally I'll drop in on and off to see how she's doing.'

Mention of the beach house would've triggered that look. Her family was wealthy. There was nothing she could do about it, but he'd never got that, had always said she had it easy when other junior doctors were studying hard and slogging their guts out, trying to make ends meet with huge loans to pay back once they qualified. Little did he know she'd paid in other ways.

Once her father had started the vineyard as

part of the farm there was the annual grape harvest, where all hands were needed, or meals to be cooked at all hours for the workers as they slogged day and night to get the grapes into the vats for her father to begin the wine-making process.

There was more than one way of being tied to financial costs and responsibilities and family. Her mother was the avoider in her family, always becoming chronically depressed when needed to help out, hence the reason Lily had fought hard to be strong and as good as her brothers on the farm. 'I want a week chilling out before starting here. After moving back to Auckland, settling into my apartment and spending time with the family, a bit of me time will work wonders on the exhaustion.'

Max's eyes were on her, giving her the once-over. Making her shiver in anticipation. Of what? No idea. He asked, 'Exhausted? Doesn't sound like the Lily Scott I once knew.'

'I'm fine. Moving, packing, getting a new job, a bit of stress, and, yes, I need time to relax. That's all.'

He stepped back. 'Good. Glad to hear it.' Then he was looking at her again. 'What stress?'

Let it go. 'Decision-making. I wanted to find the right GP position, one I could plan a future around.' Then she'd gone and joined the place where Max worked. *Good thinking, Lily. That was an amazing decision.* Except she was starting to feel it might have been and not only for the work. *It can't. Not at all.*

'Fair enough.' Max was nodding but there was still a question in his expression. Concern? For her?

It looked like it. The angst that had risen too quickly from past memories backed off. If Max could be kind to her, then she owed it to him to be equally pleasant, if not downright friendly. The past was exactly that, and tonight was the beginning of something else. Something she could make into a wonderful experience, and include Max as part of it. As medical colleagues.

A delicate shiver lifted the hairs on the back of her neck. There'd never been nights quite like the ones she'd had with this man, not before or since. She was now a free woman—who did not need a man trying to tell her how to run her life all the time, who didn't accept her for who she was. Would this Max be like that? She looked at him and couldn't find the answer.

'Here, you two. You're the only ones without a glass in your hands and we're about to have some speeches.' Devlin stood beside them, two glasses of red wine in his large hand.

'Tell me that's a Scott Merlot Cabernet,' Max laughed. 'It's my pick of NZ reds any day.'

'What else?' Devlin laughed back.

'Now I work here, you'll get a good deal on any you buy.' Lily smiled. 'That includes anyone who's interested.'

'You might live to regret that.' Max laughed again, a genuine sound with no questions behind it. 'Seriously, thank you.'

'Right, let's get this show happening before people start wandering off for a meal.' Devlin tapped his glass. 'Attention, everyone.' The room went quiet instantly. 'Sarah, come forward and let me wax lyrical about you for a moment.'

Sarah stepped up, a warm smile directed at Devlin. 'That'd be a first.'

As the laughter died down, Devlin continued. 'You've been a wonderful partner in the practice. Kept us all on our toes and created strong relationships with each of us and your patients.'

While he extolled Sarah's talents Lily looked around at the people she'd be soon start working with. Genuine fondness for Sarah showed on all the faces, and she could only hope she'd come close to replacing the GP everyone looked up to.

Drawing a deep breath, she took a sip of wine and felt a moment of insecurity. What if she wasn't up to the position? She'd done a good job in Singapore, and had come home with a superb reference, so why wouldn't she be up to the job? Devlin had head-hunted her when he'd heard from her father that she was returning home. He wouldn't have done that if she didn't have the skills and competence the partners required. But apprehension still knotted deep inside her, and she couldn't understand why. Staring into her glass as though the answer was there, she let her mind roam in search of a clue.

'Hey.' A quiet nudge from her left. Max.

The answer. It was Max shaking her up. Previously, he'd never have quietly brought her back to where she should be focused. He'd have made a joke about her lack of concentration. What else was going to be dissimilar? Working in a different environment from what she'd become used to? She thrived on challenges, but was she up to this one? And did she mean Max or the medical centre's expectations?

'Listen.' Max again, still in a quiet voice no one else would hear.

Glancing around, she found the room's focus on her, and lifted her shoulders into confident mode. Please let no one have seen that moment of worry.

'I'm happy to be handing over to you, Lily. You'll be excellent.' Sarah closed the gap between them and gave her a hug. 'I mean it,' she said quietly.

Lily returned her hug. They'd spent hours together going through their patients and sharing a couple of meals at the restaurant down the road. 'I'll do my absolute best.' To hell with the doubts looming in her head.

Devlin hadn't finished. 'Welcome, Lily. I'm so pleased you're joining us.' Then he raised his glass. 'Okay, let's have a toast to Sarah and Lily, and get on with enjoying the evening.'

As the noise level increased again, Lily stood back to watch, still shaken by her sudden concerns.

Then Max tapped his glass against hers. 'Feel like heading to Capacio's after this for a meal and catch-up?'

Max was asking her out for a meal. Not on a date surely? It would be rude to decline. But suddenly she'd had enough of getting her head around how he'd changed. He'd thrown her preconceived ideas and old memories to the wind and she was struggling. This Max seemed great, but was she rushing her acceptance that he'd changed so much? She needed space to remind herself she was not looking for a man to share her life, and especially not this one. She needed space to quieten the slow drumming in her veins, to douse the warmth filling her.

'Unfortunately I've got to see my sister-in-law, so I'll take a rain-check.' The moment the words were out she regretted them. Why not go along for some fun? It didn't have to be about

Max. But it was too late. There was no way to undo the words without appearing rude. 'Next time?'

'Sure.' By the look in his eyes there wouldn't be a next time.

CHAPTER TWO

MAX ROUNDED THE corner and braked. An SUV with flashing hazard lights was parked in the centre of the secondary road leading to the Let's Have Fun camp at the end of Whangaparaoa Peninsula. Further on, what appeared to be at least one enormous pine tree blocked all hope of further travel.

'Damn. Should've stuck with the main road.' The lure of Lily had tempted him off track, and now he was stopped almost outside her beach house. If he'd been late before this, there was no hope now of making it to the camp before the kids were out and at it. But, then, he wasn't meant to oversee them twenty-four seven, and no one expected him before ten at the earliest.

Even with the windows closed the harsh noise of chainsaws in action was loud. Two people were cutting branches off the tree, while two older men were engrossed in moving the sawn lengths to the side of the road as they came free, ready to be loaded on a trailer attached to a nearby tractor.

Stepping out and tossing his jacket onto his seat, Max shut the car and headed over to the men. Might as well make himself useful. 'Need some help?'

One man straightened up from the growing stack of timber, sweat streaming down his face despite the chilly winter air. 'Sure do, mate. We can't keep up with those two.'

Max looked over at the people wielding their machines and gaped. A pocket of heat expanded throughout his chilled body. Surely not? Then again, why not? Lily could still surprise him, which shouldn't be a surprise at all. She might be tall enough to lay her head on his shoulder but she was slim and that chainsaw wasn't made for cutting kindling. He couldn't stop looking at the apparition before him. Curvaceous in the right places, no biceps bulging from strain to fill out the sleeves of an oversized plaid work shirt unlike anything he'd seen her wear before.

'Here, put these on.' One man handed him leather work gloves and leaned close to be heard above the din. 'Saves getting splinters in your hands. Name's Archie, and this here's George. That guy over there's Cal. I'm thinking you know Lily by the stunned look on your dial.'

'I do. I'm Max.' He was still gaping at Lily as

she attacked a large branch with skill. 'What's she doing, brandishing that lethal equipment?'

'Better not let her hear you say that or you'll likely lose a leg.' Archie laughed. 'She's darned handy with a chainsaw, believe me.'

As he watched, the branch hit the ground with a thud, and Lily straightened, pushed the safety goggles off her face and turned in his direction. And blinked. 'Max?' she mouthed, surprise registering in her steady gaze. A smile appeared on her face.

'Obviously me,' he answered silently, drinking in the sight of her face. How had he never realised how beautiful her smiles were? Because she'd hardly ever smiled at him. Just as well or his gut would have become permanently cramped. Nodding, he moved closer to the destruction to begin lifting logs to carry to the trailer. The muscles in his shoulders tightened as he sensed her watching him. And tightened some more when he realised she'd left her position to come across.

'When did the trees come down?' he asked to prevent saying what was really dominating his mind.

'About five this morning. We waited for sunrise before getting stuck in. How did you manage to come this way? There's supposed to be a warning sign up at the turnoff.' Her breathing was even, despite what that chainsaw must weigh.

'Afraid not. Unless I missed it.' Anything was possible. He'd been dreaming about catching up with Lily again, and fighting the excitement that had brought on. She'd disappointed him when she'd turned down his offer to go for a meal together last Thursday. Once he'd have been irked, but not any more. It seemed those feelings had been replaced with a need to really know Lily, to get on with *her* emotions. Emotions best avoided but already impossible to ignore.

Warmth had flooded him whenever he'd thought about her over the last few days. So had the warning that he wasn't looking for love, even if he wanted it. He had no intention of hurting a woman emotionally to meet his own ends. Hell. Emotion here, there and everywhere. It hadn't used to be in his vocabulary. He blamed Lily. He smiled. Yeah, of course he did.

She smiled back. 'You're out early. Another hour and you'd have got through, no bother.'

'This will be cleared in an hour?' An exaggeration surely?

'We've already cleared another, admittedly smaller tree further along.' She grinned. 'I'd better get back to it. Are you okay doing this in those clothes? The pine's covered in sap. There are overalls in the garage behind the house if you want.' Her head dipped in the direction of the stained timber, low-build home with picture windows from end to end and glossy-leafed shrubs placed strategically around the lawn. Beautiful in its simplicity.

Max sighed. The property was a perfect match for Lily. 'I've jeans and an old shirt in the car. They'll do.' He hadn't brought good clothes for the week, preferring casual ones as it often helped kids relax when they wanted to talk about their problems. He flicked the boot catch and undid the buckle of his belt—see, no notches, Lily—and smiled to himself as she hurried back to the fallen trees. Very prudish looking when she was anything but. In bed at least. He took a deep intake of air, forced it out.

Those nights together had been a revelation. The argumentative woman had flipped a switch and been hot and exciting, giving so much of herself he'd had to wonder if there were two Lilys. Then a third had come to light afterwards when she had walked away from him and kept him at a distance with her sharp retorts to anything he'd said.

It had been a wake-up call, forcing him to stop and wonder what the hell he had been playing at. Finding he wasn't immune to her, that his heart might want to take a second look had shocked him silly. Until Lily, playing the field and remaining single had been the only way to go for him. After that, other women's reactions towards his easy come, easy go attitude had made him realise he'd been selfish. He'd got that from his mother, who'd said girls were easier to raise than boys and that Max would need his father to keep him on track while he was growing up.

First Lily and then cancer had finally taught him how important kindness and honesty were. All the while Lily had continued niggling away at him, lighting a spark in his body, long after she'd finished working at the department to head offshore. A spark that had been relit across the road outside the medical centre last week.

He'd been his father's son: tough. His mother had been right about that, but it wasn't a strength he was proud of once he'd understood he'd hurt people because of it. And he did love his dad. When he'd been young, his father had dreamed of becoming a doctor but his family had been dirt poor so the day he'd turned fifteen he had left school to find a job. At first Max had wanted to study medicine for his father, but even before he'd started training he'd known there was no other career for him. He'd found a side to himself that involved caring for people without giving away his heart.

The medical scene had absorbed him, made

him happy for the first time. He'd found his niche. Only when he'd been ill had his mother admitted being proud of him. Even his father, in his gruff way, had said so. That moment had lifted the cloud that had sat on his heart all his life. *Dad was proud of him.* And his mother.

The females in his family hadn't abandoned him entirely when he'd been young. He'd spent time with them as they'd lived only three streets away, and his step-dad had accepted him as part of his family. But he'd been determined to put on a brave face like his father had done, and not show his hurt over being left behind.

Lily had been the one exception in his life—after the fact. At first she had been no different from any other date, but soon she could have had him eating out of her hand for more of her gentleness and that off-the-scale lovemaking. Yes, lovemaking, the first and only time he'd called sex anything other than sex. For good reason. Sex didn't involve his heart. Lily had knocked on it.

It had been a game-changer. One that had had him raising the barriers to keep her out of his mind and soul. Even now he didn't understand why. More importantly, why had Lily made him feel that when they hadn't been close? He'd sometimes wondered if she too felt abandoned in some way and that he might hold some answers for her needs. Then he'd decide he was being crazy. Lily would never want him other than in the sack. It was payback for the women he'd treated the same over the years. But she'd remained an itch ever since.

The chainsaws roared to life, the sharp sound of blades cutting through wet wood filling the air. Lily and her off-sider were careful, keeping distance between themselves and continually checking to see where everyone was. The equipment wasn't something to argue with.

A vivid, gruesome picture came to Max's mind from his first year as an intern in an emergency room. He shuddered. A woodsman working in a pine forest had slipped while felling a tree and the result had not been good, the only thing saving the man from bleeding out being the other woodsmen working the same area with basic first-aid training to their credit. But the real mess had been handed over to Max and his colleagues at the hospital. They'd saved the guy's leg and he'd gone back to work in the forests as soon as he'd been able, saying it couldn't happen twice. Max wasn't so sure. Imagine if anything like that happened to Lily. No, he did not want to conjure up that hideous image. Lily handled her saw with all the confidence she'd use with a dessert spoon, only she was super-vigilant.

'She knows what she's doing.' Archie spoke beside him.

Max shuddered again. 'I'm sure she does, but it's nerve-racking to watch.'

'Learned off her old man and those brothers she pretends are as weak as kittens.' Archie chuckled. 'No one was ever going to hold Lily back. Only had to say bet she couldn't do something and she'd be off to prove them wrong.'

'There's a woman I recognise. Though she never tried to prove anyone wrong in the medical world, only determined not to make mistakes.' Just like him. They'd been more similar than he'd realised. Wonder what else they had in common he didn't know about?

'You've worked with her?'

'While we were training.'

Why hadn't he spent time getting to know her better, instead of overreacting to her confident manner, when she had made it abundantly clear she wanted nothing more to do with him? He'd acted as per normal—distant—but what if he'd wooed her with some finesse? She'd got her own back by popping into his head on and off, except in the bleakest days of his treatment, giving him a nagging sense of a missed opportunity for something wonderful. He'd never know what that was about. Unless… Unless nothing. That'd mean letting her in to get behind the shield keeping his heart safe. How was he going to avoid that *and* get to know her better?

When both chainsaws finally stopped, the silence was overwhelming. Lily swiped her hands on her overalls, highlighting her shapely hips. Max swallowed a groan, squashed the stab of longing hitting him.

'We're done,' Lily called. 'Let's haul the last of this clear of the road and go have a coffee, everyone.'

'Best thing I've heard all morning.' He should head away and find the camp, not hang out with Lily and her old cronies, except the idea of staying on for a bit warmed him. Max lifted a log up onto his shoulder and headed for the trailer.

Looking around, he breathed in the cold air tightening his skin and absorbed the sound of waves crashing onto the shore beyond the road. The air was heavy with salt and above gulls shrieked as they dived and soared while they patrolled the beach. Calm overtook Max. This was a great location for a week away from the madness that was the medical hub. No wonder Lily had come here before starting work.

'I can even run to bacon and eggs if you're lucky, guys.' Lily was speaking to them all but smiling directly at him.

He could return her refusal to join him the other night, show her he wasn't moved by her reappearing in his life, but it wasn't in him to say no.

She'd stung his pride when he'd thought they'd been getting on well, yet there was a warmth tucking around him he hadn't known for a long time, and he was damned if he could shuck it off. It felt good, right, and he wanted more. *Careful*. Damn, but he was tired of being careful. Again, it was Lily upsetting his determination to remain single, to cruise through life without involving, and thereby hurting, someone else. Lily. Gulp. *Lily?* Being careful was so ingrained in him, yet within days—in a blink—of catching sight of Lily again and 'careful' was disappearing from his vocabulary. Dangerous. For her. For him.

The month of isolation to prevent catching anyone's germs when his system had had no resistance due to the new treatment. The weeks after chemo when he hadn't wanted anyone to see him looking so despondent—not to mention bald, though that had been quite funny when the cause didn't tear him apart.

Now that gnawing fear of the cancer returning made him leery of getting involved with someone and having to watch them cope, to pick up the pieces afterwards if the worst happened, of breaking their heart along with his. It wasn't the greatest place to be, keeping a space between himself and everyone else, especially someone who could make all the difference if she was prepared to accept he didn't have a guaranteed future.

Lighten up. You've only just caught up with Lily and you're thinking all this? Get real. Get practical. 'Got mushrooms to go with that?'

One well-styled eyebrow rose. 'The man wants it all.'

Did he ever. Max shrugged, trying to keep that to himself. 'Tomatoes?'

'Thought you knew this woman,' Archie grunted as he dragged a log the length of his body off the road.

'Here, let me take that.' Max leapt after him and took the heavy load from the old man. 'Can't have you falling on your face because Lily didn't cut that in two.'

'My fault, eh? Let me take the other end, Max.' She took hold of the log and headed for the trailer, leaving Max no choice but to follow or drop the wood on his toes.

'It wasn't a challenge,' he muttered, thinking how Archie had said she always took those on.

'No, it's about saving Archie's face. And heart,' she added quietly as they set their load on the trailer. 'He's got arrhythmia.'

'Which explains the heavy breathing.' He'd wanted to ask Archie about that but had got the evil eye when he'd opened his mouth. 'Tough old guy, isn't he?'

'Yes, which is better than sitting in his rocking chair all day.'

'Can't do that any more,' Archie butted in. 'No newspapers these days.'

'What's wrong with the internet?' Max asked cheekily.

'You have to ask? I remember when we had party lines on our phones. Phones that were stuck to the wall and you couldn't wander around the place yabbering your head off in front of everyone.'

'You've got me on that one.' Max shook his head. 'There's something to be said for modern technology and getting medical test results when they're done, not the next day in the mail. Not to mention keeping in touch with friends when you can't see them.'

Like in hospital in the middle of the night when fear of the future was tracking around your head and there was no way to stop it without talking to someone who knew you.

George had joined them. 'You can keep track of your woman all the time.'

If he had one he'd be in touch, and available, not keeping tabs on her. 'Never. I still believe in privacy.' His gaze went to the tidy shoulders of the woman in front of him. She was a private person. Once he'd mistakenly believed it was snobbery because she didn't blab about herself as some other women did. Watching her work the room during the party the other night, he'd realised he'd got that wrong.

'Ten minutes and we're finished here.' Lily reached for a smaller chunk of pine.

Max picked up a piece. 'I can smell the bacon already.'

'George, Archie, you going to join us?' Lily asked hopefully. 'Cal?'

'Thanks, but I'd better get home and see why Enid hasn't been over with a cuppa like she promised. Probably engrossed in some book and forgotten all about us.' Archie added his load to the trailer. 'There's a fair whack of fire wood here.'

'I'll cut it up over the next few days and bring it across.' Lily nodded.

'You'll split the large rounds?' Max asked. Lily might be tough but she wasn't built like one of those axemen in the wood-chopping contests.

'If there's no one else to do it, I'll cheat and use the chainsaw. It does make a mess but I'm not into body building.'

'Glad to hear it.' Her figure couldn't be faulted. She certainly didn't need muscles on top of muscles filling the sleeves of her shirts. 'You might lose a toe or two.'

'Careful,' Cal growled. 'That's a challenge to Lily.'

He laughed. 'Lily, ignore me.'

'I am.' Her smile was wide and full of fun.

And hit him where he didn't want to be hit. In his heart. He gasped, looked away. Not his heart. More likely in that roped-down centre that kept him on the straight and narrow leading into the future, fuelled by a need to concentrate on those he could help through medicine and not ask for anything back. But he didn't want to be ignored by Lily. Not by anybody. But especially not Lily. Even in jest.

'Park your car in the driveway, out of the way,' Lily told Max, before climbing onto the tractor and flicking on the engine, drowning out his reply. He'd surprised her by leaping in to help when he'd realised what they were doing. Her family had taught her that—jump in and help, no questions asked. Her back complained when she looked over her shoulder while backing her load around. Tomorrow all her body would ache from the exertion of cutting those trees. The chainsaw was made for heavy work, not weekenders wanting to tidy their yard, and her arms would know about it for days to come, but right now she felt alive and buzzing.

Being physical always hyped her up. *Max*

hypes you up. There was no denying that. Strange how any time he was around her blood hummed and hope started rearing its head. But they weren't going to get closer. They couldn't. A sigh trickled over her lips. She wasn't going there. There were only so many knocks a girl could take.

The men strode up the drive, tugging gloves off their hands and pausing to wait for Max to park and step out of his car.

Lily watched him straighten, roll those broad shoulders and look around until he found her and smiled. Sent the blood racing through her veins. Focusing on the job on hand and not Max, she positioned the trailer under the trees for some shelter from any precipitation in the coming days. The forecast was for scattered showers, but around here everyone knew to be prepared for rain any time.

Then, breathing deeply, she feigned nonchalance and strolled to the back door, calling out, 'I'm putting the kettle on. Archie, try to convince Enid to join us.'

'I'll sling her over my shoulder and bring her across.' Archie headed for the stile over the fence between their properties.

As he unlaced his shoes on the back step, Max asked, 'Can I give you a hand with breakfast?'

Used to getting on with things by herself, Lily hesitated. Max sounded genuine in his offer. This relaxed feeling between them felt right. 'Absolutely. Come on in, guys, and make yourselves comfortable. Bathroom's along there.' She pointed to the hallway on the right for Max's benefit. 'Or there's a hand basin in the laundry.'

Tossing her jacket on a peg inside the back door, she headed to the kitchen. Strong coffee was what she needed more than anything. And for Max to change his mind and get on the road to the camp so she could breathe again. The moment she'd seen him standing by his car her heartbeat had gone haywire and still wasn't settling.

He'd taken the long way round to the camp and had ended up pretty much at her front door. At the family beach-house door, if she was nitpicking. Had he deliberately set out to find her? If so, she wasn't sure how that made her feel.

The restlessness that had gripped her since Leo had left, taking her dream of a family with him, hadn't gone away completely. A need to settle in her own home and have a great job had bought her apartment and got the job of a lifetime, but there was still a hole in her life. Love. A man and a family. After her relationship failures she struggled with getting out there to find a man who might be the love of her life, but having a baby was still as clear as ever.

She'd researched surrogacy, had had an initial consultation at the fertility clinic in Remuera. The next step was as high as a mountain.

Having a baby would be amazing, life-altering in the best way imaginable. Her heart was full of love to give. It was choosing a father that gave her concern. Using a sperm bank was too impersonal for something so special and close. Babies should come not only into love but from love. She'd prefer a man she knew and admired to volunteer, not a number from the fertility bank. It might be a long wait to sort this out, but there was no rush. She wanted to settle into her job first anyway.

A long, sad sigh filled the kitchen. Hers. Startled, she glanced around, relieved to find herself alone. It was time to focus on feeding the men then getting on with the day, including catching up with Josie.

'Where can I start?' Max stepped into the light and airy kitchen dining space and instantly the room felt smaller.

And warmer. Lily hugged herself before turning around. 'Knowing these men, a hot drink will be essential first. You'll find mugs in that cupboard, tea, etcetera over on that shelf.' Clicking the gas on to heat the elements, she removed pans from a drawer under the bench and went to the fridge for eggs and bacon.

'I'll set the table.' George was already opening the cutlery drawer.

Lily loved these men. They'd been a part of her summer holidays most of her life; their children friends to catch up with in summer when everyone had come for Christmas and New Year and to recharge their batteries. 'Cal, this is Max Bryant, a GP and sports doctor at the medical centre I'm starting at next week.'

Max shook the man's hand. 'I've come out to attend the camp and help any poor kid that can't find someone better.'

'Guess you'll have time to split that wood, then.' Cal chuckled.

'Probably.' Max grinned. Then got serious. 'From what I hear, the kids are already resilient and determined to have a lot of fun doing all the activities. I've been told there'll be a few pulled muscles and aches from overdoing some of the challenges, but otherwise nothing major.'

'Don't speak too soon,' Lily warned, ducking around Max in the small space, focused on not bumping into that hot body. 'We've already had a broken leg this year at an earlier camp. An eight-year-old girl with one leg climbed a tree. All good, and to be encouraged to a point, but in this case the branch she was on broke.'

'Along with said leg.' Max shook his head. 'Kids, eh?'

'Exactly. We take a lot of precautions, but we also want them to have fun doing the things their counterparts do, like climb trees and leap over fences and fall in the duck pond. It's normal, and that's what they need more than anything. To be normal.' Lily stopped. 'Sorry, that sounds like I'm lecturing, and I didn't mean to.'

Max nodded. 'It's fine. I get it. It's how you'd have grown up on the farm and how I was in town, always at some park or beach, running riot.' As he added boiling water to the coffee plunger, he said, 'You keep saying "we" when referring to the camp. What's your role in the place?'

That's what happened when she relaxed—she gave too much away. 'Being on the board of directors, I tend to keep an eye on everything.'

'Even when you were living overseas?'

Why had George and Cal chosen this moment to stop talking to each other? She couldn't divert Max to whatever they'd been discussing, though knowing those two it would be about their backaches or stiff knees so wouldn't have been much help. 'I oversaw the set-up and haven't stepped aside since.' The site had been chosen for the rundown motel that stood in the middle of a large area of flat land leading to the beach. An extensive makeover, along with building further accommodation buildings, adding a communal kitchen, dining room and an activities hall had completed the camp. She'd paid for it all.

'Anything to do with Josie?'

He didn't miss a thing.

'Some. She's been luckier than most kids in her situation. Growing up on the farm with my brother for her dad meant she wasn't held back, instead encouraged to get out and do the chores and ride the pony, dig a posthole. I saw what other kids could gain from sampling something similar.'

'It wouldn't only be her dad egging her on. Her aunt's never been one to sit back and feel sorry for herself.'

You don't know a thing, Max. Or nothing that matters. 'I've been known to nudge her along at times.'

Cal roared with laughter. 'Like making Josie fill the trailer with sand for the pétanque court around the side of the house.'

'And did she do a great job?' Lily grinned. She hadn't bullied Josie at all, instead she'd been told she was mean for not letting Josie do the job in the first place.

'She did, and is still proud of herself.'

'Lily, will you come and see Enid?' Archie burst into the kitchen, looking rattled.

'What's up?' Lily moved up to him.

'She's speaking funny and can't move her leg and arm on one side.'

Enid never had a sick day, and adored getting out and about in the garden when she wasn't reading the stack of books by her bedside. 'I'll grab my bag.'

Max flicked off the gas and put aside the pans that had been heating. 'Archie, lead the way while Lily gets her gear.'

'I can't make head or tail of what she's saying.'

Lily bit her lip. *Sounds like a stroke.*

Max's eyes met Lily's over Archie's head, acknowledgement coming her way. They were on the same page.

She dashed to her bedroom for the medical kit and her cellphone.

'We'll get out of the way,' George said.

One look at Enid a few minutes later and Lily was tapping her phone. The left side of her face was contorted and while her lips were moving her speech was gibberish. 'I'm calling the rescue helicopter.'

Max was kneeling by the bed, talking quietly. 'Enid, I'm Max, a doctor and a friend of Lily's. Archie says you were reading when he went out to help with the fallen trees this morning.'

Enid's right eye widened briefly.

'That's a yes?'

Another slight movement in the eyelid.

'How long do you think you've been lying here like this? One hour?'

No movement.

'More?'

No movement.

'That might be good,' Lily muttered. Enid might be in the golden hour. Or she could've been like this for a lot longer. They'd been working on those trees for at least three hours.

'Emergency service. Do you require the ambulance, police or fire service?'

'Ambulance,' Lily answered briskly.

Max asked, 'Archie, what time did you head outside to help Lily and the men?'

'I think it was about six but I can't be sure. What's wrong with Enid? She can hear you. Sort of answers you.'

'It was near six,' Lily said.

'Ambulance service. Please tell me the nature of your call.'

'I'm Lily Scott, a GP. We're on the Whangaparaoa Peninsula and I have a woman who appears to have had a stroke. There's a possibility we're in the golden hour so I suggest sending the rescue helicopter.'

'I need some details, Dr Scott. Bear with me for a moment.'

'There're two doctors here.' It was irritating to go through this when she was a doctor, but she understood the reasons behind the system. Answering the questions quickly and getting information from Max, Lily waited while the woman at the other end put her on hold.

'Archie.' Max looked up at the man. 'We think Enid's had a stroke. Can you tell me if she's got any medical conditions and if she takes any medications?'

'What? A stroke? No, not that. Enid, look at me, tell me you're all right.' He was shaking and gasping for air.

Lily stepped around the bed and wrapped an arm around his shoulders. 'Archie, deep breath in. Let it out. That's it. We're getting Enid urgent help now. Max is checking everything. She's in good hands. I want you to sit down by the bed and hold Enid's other hand. Concentrate on breathing properly. You're no help to her if you get wound up.' She pulled the chair from the dressing table across and gently pushed Bill onto it just as the emergency dispatcher came back on the line.

'Dr Scott, the rescue helicopter is on the way. Is there somewhere safe to land close by?'

'There's an expansive grassed area in front of the houses in this bay. I'll arrange for neighbours to be out there to wave when the helicopter gets here, and to keep the area clear of vehicles and people. There're some wind gusts after last night's storm from the south east.'

'I'll pass on the information. Since Enid has doctors in attendance I won't keep you on the line, but call back if there're any concerns.'

'Just get that rescue team here fast.' She hung up, knowing she hadn't needed to say that, but had been unable to stop herself. This was personal. She and Max were doing all they could but Enid needed to be in hospital. 'Helicopter's on the way, Archie. Max, I need to get George and Cal to head to the reserve and keep it clear.'

'Of course. It's a long shot but you haven't got breathing equipment in the house, by any chance?' Max asked.

She shook her head. 'Sorry.'

That bad, eh? Her heart stuttered for Archie and Enid. *Hang in there, Enid. Help's on its way.*

'I'll be back as quickly as possible.' Max had it covered, but heading outside when this was going on went against all she'd trained for, even though organising people to make it easier for the chopper to land was helping just as much.

'I could do that if you want to stay here,' Max offered.

He understood her need to be there for her neighbours. 'Thank you, but I know where I'm going and I'll be back fast.' She headed outside, leaping the fence and dashing through a back yard to get to George's house. 'George, where are you? We need help.'

As soon as George grasped what she was saying, he insisted on organising everything and sent her back to Enid. She left immediately, needing to be on the spot, not away from Enid and Archie. And Max. 'Really?' she gasped, as she raced through the back yard. Yes, really. This Max was stronger in a kind, caring way.

'How's Enid?' Lily asked the moment she stepped into the bedroom, and immediately wished she'd kept her mouth shut. She knew there'd be no change, definitely not for the better and probably not at all.

'I shouldn't have gone out to shift those trees.' Archie was stricken.

Lily went to hug him. There was nothing she could say. It was natural to blame himself, even when he couldn't have known Enid was in trouble.

Max gave her a tight smile as he continued monitoring Enid's heart and breathing, noting everything down. An eternity seemed to pass before the thumping of helicopter rotors came from directly above the house.

As the machine moved towards the reserve and hovered, Lily was holding her breath, begging them in her mind to hurry while understanding the need for caution. The paramedics would be here as soon as they could. Which was never fast enough. She hugged Archie again, her eyes fixed on Enid, wondering how much she understood.

Suddenly the room was crowded with paramedics and their equipment. Lily and Max were redundant. Outside a stretcher stood ready for loading Enid. Max said, 'It's hard to hand over, isn't it? Even when the paramedics are better equipped, it goes against all I feel about helping people.'

'It's difficult,' she agreed.

Max looked at her. 'I'm sorry about your friends.'

She teared up. Slashing her hand across her face, she muttered, 'I know people will say Enid's in her early seventies, it was to be expected something would happen one day. But I've known these two over half my life and Enid still gets around, doing the garden and cooking and going to group meetings.' Sniff. 'Am I writing her off already?'

A firm hand settled on her shoulder, pulled her close to that safe chest. 'That's no small stroke she's suffered but, as we both know, there's no telling for sure what's ahead until all the tests have been completed.'

Max was only saying what she knew, but it helped somehow. As did the warmth from his body pervading her senses and taking away the loneliness that had started coming over her. 'Thanks.' She wasn't in a hurry to move away.

One of the paramedics appeared to take the stretcher inside.

'Need a hand?' Max stepped back, leaving her chilled.

'That'd be great. Two of us can carry this and someone take our gear.'

'Where will you take Enid?' Lily asked as she followed them.

'North Shore General Hospital. Will someone be driving the husband down?'

'I will.' It was a no-brainer.

Except in the end George and Cal insisted on taking him. 'We're his mates, we go through everything together,' George pointed out.

'I get it,' she agreed. Who else would Archie want in this situation, except those nearest and dearest to him? 'Keep me posted.'

As the chopper rose from the reserve, Lily started back to the beach house. 'I really need that coffee.'

'Mind if I join you?' Max asked.

'I expected you to,' she replied. 'Still on for breakfast?' Her appetite was returning. No surprise there.

'You have to ask?' He smiled.

A smile that touched her, and had her wondering about the warmth returning throughout her. Her wariness was backing off. It wasn't as though they'd have another fling. Definitely not. 'That's a yes, then.' Her next sigh was crisper. Her body was tightening. Good looking, in great physical shape, Max had a way of looking at her that made her toes curl, but they were not getting hooked up again. He'd only hurt her in the end, and anyway she wasn't about to change her mind and start testing the dating waters. Whatever happened, she couldn't get involved with Max.

CHAPTER THREE

MAX GRIMACED. 'MICHELLE'S doing everything possible for her injuries, and more, but the mind games aren't helping.'

'That's to be expected,' Lily said.

'Yes, but she hasn't got this far with her career by feeling sorry for herself.' Lily didn't know Michelle yet. 'There've been times when she's had to toughen up and face reality, whether it was not being chosen for the team earlier or making a mess of a game plan during a match. She works hard, has gone without a social life to be out there keeping up peak fitness levels. Her medical records show a couple of instances when she's overdone things, but there's no mention of feeling down.'

'She might've kept that to herself.' Lily looked at him with determination. 'I've got an idea.'

'Go on,' he answered slowly, already with an inkling of where this was headed, and not sure if it was right for his patient. Their patient, he reminded himself.

'We could suggest she comes to the camp for a day or two to help the kids find their confidence in areas they're uncertain about. Whether it's a different sport or a hobby they might want to learn, she could encourage them with the strength she's used to become successful in netball.'

'You think that would work when she's feeling flat? She might pass on negative thoughts, not encouraging ones.' As he saw Lily's eyes light up, he shrugged, denying the laughter that wanted to escape at her persistence. That was Lily to a T. 'That's what you'd put to her when, in fact, you think the children might help her get her mojo back.'

Lily smiled, and went back to flipping bacon. 'Just a thought. Could work for everyone.'

'It might.' Max weighed the benefits and the negatives, not that he could think of anything against the idea other than Michelle getting more frustrated than ever. Except he didn't think she would. Once she accepted what had happened and began moving forward she'd start looking around to see what her next step was. No wonder he loved his job. He helped people through bad times.

'The kids are usually full of enthusiasm and

when the going gets tough they either dig deep or turn for help. That's where she could benefit them, and in turn get something back, watching kids facing long-term difficulties and not losing hope.'

'We'll both talk to her,' Max decided. 'You should put the proposal to her as you're a part of the camp's hierarchy.' Lily started to shake her head. 'Wait. You're new to her medical life and she likes you so she'll listen.'

'You're saying she wouldn't take any notice if you outlined the idea?' The doubt in her voice was strong. 'Come on.'

Lily understood him well. It was unbelievable, and wonderful. He could get too comfortable with this. 'She'd listen, but she might also look at the idea from every way, trying to find what's behind it, whereas coming from you it will be new and intriguing. I've had a lot to do with Michelle's sports side of things in the past year and I think I understand her.' The toaster popped and he placed the toast onto a plate on the table, put two more slices of bread in to toast. 'Anyway, it was your idea.'

'Fine. We'll call her after breakfast and see how she reacts. You'll be better able to read her. If you don't mind,' she added a little tersely.

'Let's get step one out of the way first.' He already knew Michelle would be take on the challenge. 'That being breakfast,' he added, trying to put aside the irritation he felt about Lily's way of seeing straight through him. She did it too easily. Now he had to focus on saving his heart, and while Lily wouldn't want his, he should be safe, but every time he saw her or heard that soft lilting voice, doubt rolled over him, making him wonder if he was more than happy she was back in his life.

How was it he could tell patients to move on to get over what'd devastated them, and not do the same for himself? Other cancer survivors said eventually a lot of the dread backed off and there'd come a time when he'd forget some of the raw fear that had smothered him. It was true to an extent, but he had a way to go.

'You burning that toast?' A sharp nudge in his side stopped his worries head on, replacing them with need for Lily and her soft, warm body.

Banging the cancel button, he snatched the blackened slices and dumped them in a small bucket labelled chook food. 'I'll try again.'

'Where were you?' Lily asked.

'You don't want to know.' Except she might. He didn't want to tell her about his doubts and needs. Though the day would come when he would have to mention the cancer as most of the doctors at the centre knew and he'd prefer Lily to find out from him.

He liked to underline how well he was and how lucky to be able to get on with his life. In other words, he didn't want people feeling sorry for him. He hated it when anyone's face filled with pity. If Lily reacted that way, he'd feel let down. Pity when they'd once taken no prisoners with each other would hurt, make him feel a little unloved, like when his mother had left him. Which was way over the top. The Lily of old would have been more likely to make a sharp retort about moving on and let the subject drop. He wasn't sure about her now.

'Maybe I do.' She served up the bacon and eggs.

He should tell her, get it done with. It wasn't a big deal. He'd been ill, had come out the other side, and was creating a lifestyle and future he was comfortable with, if he ignored his longing for love and family. If he ignored the doubts he couldn't quite get past about the future. Sitting down at the table, he reached for the plate of bacon and eggs. Suddenly he needed to be heading to the camp, away from Lily with all the confusion she brought on, and an intense physical longing that was like an elbow in the ribs.

'Right.'

The only sound was cutlery on plates. The

silence between them reminded Max of the post-fling days when they'd spoken only when necessary. But if he tried too hard to get on-side with her, he'd be letting Lily in closer than ever, and that could not happen. He was vulnerable to her. Accepting that, he'd take it on the chin and do his best to ignore the ache in his gut. As soon as he'd rinsed the dishes and placed them in the dishwasher he looked up and found Michelle's number. 'Ready?'

'Yes.'

They listened to the ringing and finally a subdued Michelle answered. 'Hi, Max.'

'Hello. I've got Lily Scott with me and we're on speaker phone. That okay?'

'I suppose.'

Glancing at Lily, he raised one eyebrow.

She nodded back, looking concerned but determined. 'Michelle, I've got an idea to put to you.' She wasn't wasting any time.

Max got in quickly, before their patient could veto things without knowing what this was about. 'Hear Lily out before you make a decision.'

'You're sounding serious.'

'We are. You need to focus on getting well, and I believe Lily's idea will go some way to helping achieve that.'

'I'm all ears.' She sounded anything but.

'Michelle, have you heard of the Let's Have Fun camp for disabled children?'

'Isn't that where Max is working this week? He said something about being away if I needed medical attention.'

'Yes. It's situated on the Whangaparaoa Peninsula and we hold regular camps for kids from around New Zealand. A group aged between ten and fifteen moved in this morning for the coming week. They'll play sports and do other activities to stretch their minds and build confidence.' Lily paused, glanced at him.

He mouthed, 'Go on.'

'I thought that since you're free this week you might like to help out, encourage kids who are struggling. You know what to say or do, and I can't think of a better inspiration for these children than someone who's done so well in her sports career.'

'You're forgetting I can't move without crutches and that I'm no longer going to England with the netball team.'

'Not at all. Those are the reasons I believe you're in a strong position to show that accidents happen and yet you still get up and keep on moving.'

Silence.

Max held his breath. He wanted to add his

bit, throw in some encouragement, but Lily had it under control.

Lily stared at the phone as though willing Michelle to give the right answer, her fingers crossed on both hands.

Finally the sound of a long indrawn breath reached them. 'Max? What do you think?'

Lily fixed her eyes on him, daring him to let Michelle off the hook.

'It's an opportunity to help these kids.' Might as well push all the buttons. 'Is there someone who could drive you out here? You can stay a day or all week. Your call.'

'Mum would give me a lift, if I wanted to come.'

'Why wouldn't you?' Lily asked.

Straight for the jugular. Max smiled. There was no backing down when Lily wanted something badly enough. Could she ever be that determined about him? What did she think about him these days?

'I'm not sure I have anything to offer those kids. They're far more used to their situations than I'll ever be,' Michelle came back sharply.

'Maybe, but there're times when they're overwhelmed and need encouragement, and to get that from someone who's working on getting through her own change of circumstances has to be of benefit.' Lily drew a breath. 'My niece has spina bifida and I've watched her achieve so much. She's confident and hates the word "can't" but still has moments of a complete lack of self-reliance.'

Don't we all? Max wondered. His illness had chipped away at his confidence for the future, even when the facts said he was probably better off than others already. The five-year sign-off couldn't come soon enough and yet would he ever be able to let go the fear of cancer returning? Or was this how he'd always be, overreacting to stomach cramps or a headache? 'Give the idea some serious thought, Michelle. I'll call you back later this morning.'

Lily glared at him. That was not how she wanted to approach this. But Michelle always thought things through before acting, never jumped in without looking.

'I'll be there tomorrow morning, bright and early. If I decide to stay over, is there a room I can have?'

Lily gaped at him, shaking her head. Then she relaxed, smiled softly as though he'd given her a present, and answered Michelle. 'The camp's full as some parents are staying too, but we'll find you somewhere to doss down.'

'I've brought the camp up on screen. It looks amazing. Are you staying there, Lily?'

'I'm staying a kilometre away, and will be

dropping in often. My niece's attending and I like spending time with her.'

'Cool. Then I guess I'll see you both tomorrow. Bye.'

Max and Lily stared at each other. 'Did that really happen?' he asked.

Lily burst out laughing. 'I think so.' She pumped her fist, then high-fived him. Even briefly her hand felt good against his. 'I can't quite believe it. Thought we'd lost her when you told her to think about it.' Lily crossed to fill the kettle. 'Another coffee?'

He'd love one. And to spend more time with Lily. Especially when she was smiling. Those smiles touched a place inside he'd kept isolated for a long time. Since the day his mother and sister had left. Dangerous. Tempting. Frightening. He stood. 'No, thanks. I'll get along to the camp and make myself known. Hopefully no one will need my medical skills, and require only encouragement and gentle coaxing to push themselves.'

Her smile vanished. 'No problem.'

There was. He stood slowly, reluctant to leave. But his heart was expanding, warming him, softening his ability to remain solitary. His fingers itched with need for her. His foot rose. He shoved it down hard on the tiles. He might feel like getting that close, but there was a lot to consider. Glancing across to the doorway, he had to trust his feet to get him out of there without upsetting Lily. Or himself. Pulling on his don't-mess-with-me face when he was in a right state internally, he said, 'Let me know when you hear how Enid is, will you?'

'Of course.' Lily nodded. 'I'll see you later at the camp.'

Outside goose-bumps rose on his arms as the chilly air struck his feverish skin. Time to get on with what he'd come up here to do, and that wasn't falling for Lily.

'Enid had a stroke.' Archie sounded defeated.

'We thought that would be the diagnosis,' Lily said. 'I'm really sorry, Archie.' Enid was in for a long recuperation, but at least she had that chance. It wouldn't be easy at her age. Enid had often said she never wanted to be reliant on other people for any reason and now she was.

'The doctors say she'll be able to move and talk again, but it'll take time.'

'These things do. She's going to rely on you a lot.'

'I'll be everything I can for her.'

'I know you will. Everyone will be there for you both as well.' Lily chatted until Archie said he had to get back to his wife. 'Talk again.'

Finishing the call, she looked around for

something to do that didn't involve a chainsaw because since Max had left so abruptly she had the urge to wreck something. It'd been as though he'd suddenly had enough of her and wanted to get away. He needn't worry. She wouldn't be hanging around the camp, trying to catch his attention. She would see how the kids were faring, and help out when they were playing team games, not follow him around like a besotted puppy, watching his expressions, wondering how being a sports doctor fitted his ambitions better than being a top-notch surgeon.

Max might have walked out of here, but his scent was in the air, his presence lightening an already sunny room. No wonder her body heated and tightened. Being near him, hearing his voice and making him laugh was starting to drive her crazy with longing. So much for being wary of romance. Except she had to keep caution in place. Aaron had left her. Leo had left her. She wasn't good at relationships.

But why was she thinking about Max when their history wasn't great? Why did she even feel like she wanted to be with him? Because she couldn't help herself. On impulse, she checked her file on the week's camp crew, found Max's number and put it in her contacts, then tapped the screen, humming as she waited for him to answer. 'Hi, I've been talking to Archie. Enid did have a stroke.' She gave him the scant details. 'It's going to be a trying time for them.'

'What about family? Will they be around to help?'

'Their son and daughter live on the peninsula. They're a close family.'

'That's a plus.' He paused, and she waited for him to hang up. Instead he said, 'I've already met most of the kids, including Josie. Talk about looking like you. There's a fire in her belly to get on with anything that comes her way, isn't there?' Admiration lightened his voice.

'She's a toughie.' Her stomach softened. Max was unlike the men she'd previously fallen for. Stronger, more reliable, with a knack of making her feel special. Could he be the father for her baby? *Gah.* Where had that come from? They didn't know each other well enough to be thinking that. She shivered. *Getting way ahead of yourself, Lily.*

'You still coming along to the camp today?'

'I'll drop by to see what everyone's up to, and check with Logan that there're no problems.' Logan ran the camp and knew what he was doing, yet she couldn't help staying in touch. Control freak? Her mouth flattened. 'Maybe I should leave him to it,' she gasped. 'It's not as though he hasn't done this often.'

Max laughed. 'He's already asked if I knew

when you might make an appearance. When I explained how your morning had panned out he said he'd call you when he had a free moment.'

She soaked up Max's relaxed attitude, relishing the warmth filling her and driving away that need to wreck something. 'So he didn't pull a face and suggest I stay away?'

'Would you?'

'Mostly. Mainly I want to catch up with Josie.' Lily found herself smiling. This happier side had been a long time in hiding, and letting it out for an airing felt so good. *Thanks, Max.* Was it because they were getting on better than before? Or did she feel there was something there she wanted to nurture between them? Was that sense of something deeper she'd experienced during their fling making a comeback? Or was she just getting on with her life and starting to enjoy herself again? Whatever the reason, bring it on. She was ripe for some fun and adventure. Just not of the heart involvement variety. She'd save that for her baby.

'I'd better go and look useful. There's a get-together of everyone after lunch followed by soccer and netball games.'

Sounded about right. 'See you later.' Now what? The kitchen was tidy, she'd talked to Archie and Max, had decided not to go to the camp just yet, and the idea of curling up with her book wasn't appealing. Her nerves had calmed. She no longer felt inclined to create havoc. Under the tree sat the trailer full of pine. Sometime it needed to be cut into firebox lengths and split in half to be left to weather before being stacked under cover. Might as well start on the lengths. Someone else would do the splitting as wielding an axe was not her thing.

'Auntie Lily, where have you been? I've been waiting for you.' Josie threw herself out of the wheelchair at Lily. 'The doctor says he knows you.' She tipped her head back to lock eyes with her. 'He's nice.'

Max could charm any female from two to ninety years old. Including herself, it seemed. 'We worked together before I went to Singapore.' She held Josie against her, breathing in her youthfulness.

'You're going to be at the same medical centre from now on.'

Okay, she could be a rascal, this one. Easing her hold, Lily let Josie stand. There was a cheeky grin on her niece's face that she understood all too well. 'Stop right there, my girl. I don't need you attempting to organise my life. I make a big enough mess of it all by myself.' She grinned. 'What have you been up to?'

'Apart from asking Dr Max lots of questions? I played netball and shot two goals.' Pride brightened her eyes.

'Not bad, huh?' She high-fived Josie's hand. 'What are the other kids like? Anyone you know?'

Crimson colour poured into Josie's cheeks. 'Um, yeah. Ollie from last time's here. I knew he was coming. We text.'

Lifting one eyebrow, Lily grinned again. 'You don't say. I'm going to have to get the chain and padlock from the shed.'

'As of now you're no longer my favourite aunt.' Josie sank back into her chair and chewed her fingernail, before looking up and laughing. 'He looks gorgeous, better than before.'

Great. Should she tell her brother and sister-in-law? Or just keep a covert eye on things and let Josie get on with being a normal teen when it wasn't always so easy for her? Lily sighed. She already knew the answer. Josie was here for a good time, which included normality and fun and learning to be more resilient than most kids their age. Not that her niece wasn't already strong, but there was no such thing as too much resilience to the things life threw at people. 'Take care, that's all I'm asking.'

'Yes, Auntie.' Josie pulled a face then laughed. 'This is me you're talking to. Your super-careful niece, remember?'

'Don't you mean my try-anything, give-it-a-go niece?' Lily retorted, and heard a deep chuckle behind her.

'You two are so alike it's surreal,' Max said.

More than he realised, Lily conceded as she felt her face grow warm. 'Family genes,' she muttered for lack of anything better to say.

'Hey, Dr Max. Lily was telling me...' Josie faltered to a stop as Lily glared at her. 'Um, that I need to go find out what I'm doing tonight.' She wheeled away before Lily could say anything to stop her.

'Little minx,' Lily muttered. 'Except she's not so little or young any more.'

'She's already shown she's a leader in the netball arena,' Max acknowledged. 'The boys can't keep their eyes off her either, and that has nothing to with netball.'

'That's all they'd better be touching her with,' Lily growled, then sighed. 'Listen to me, sounding more like her parents than her fun aunt.'

'Could be you remember what you got up to at that age.'

She loved it when he joked with her. 'Isn't that how parents think? I wonder how I'd cope being a parent. Teenagers can be such trouble.' The good humour bubbled inside her. Babies grew into kids then teenagers. It was part of the deal, and she wanted it all. She'd be fine. Love coped with most things.

'You don't mean that,' Max said with a hint of sadness darkening his features. 'Having children is most people's dream.'

'Max? Why do you sound dejected all of a sudden?' she asked without thought. She didn't like to see him like this. Didn't want him hurting. Was it a dream of his to have kids that he couldn't meet?

He shook his head abruptly and looked out towards the beach. 'Nothing.'

It wasn't true. His suddenly slumped shoulders backed her conviction she'd touched on something hurtful. Not that they were close and would swap tales of woe but, 'You know where to find me if you ever want to vent. There's always wine to go with that.' *And arms to hold you.*

Slowly he turned to look at her, astonishment quickly replaced with relief. 'Thanks for being understanding.'

'It's not hard. We all get our share of knocks.'

'You, too?'

'Of course. And I'm not being flippant.'

'For once I wish you were. I don't like thinking you've been hurt, Lily.'

Yeah, well. 'It's part of being human. But I'm here, content.' She paused. That was so true it was almost laughable. 'And looking forward to the rest of the week.'

The sadness shadowing Max's eyes lifted. 'Me, too.' Did his intense gaze suggest she take that any way she chose?

Warmth tripped over her skin. Then she did something she couldn't believe. Slipping her arm through his, she said, 'Come on. Logan wants to chat to us both about Michelle's role.' Glancing up for his reaction, Lily smiled. Being this close to Max gave her inexplicable hope. The future was brightening, the darkness fading, just when she'd decided to give men a miss for a while.

Under her hand Max tensed then swiftly relaxed again and began walking with her towards the office-cum-staffroom. 'Funny, he didn't say anything to me earlier.'

'There's probably a lot going on in his head at the moment. The first day is always crazy busy.'

'I'm beginning to understand just how important this place is to you.' Those intense eyes returned to her.

'Very.' She had no idea why, but she wanted to be open with him. The need to share was grabbing her, no matter what his reaction might be. Unused to telling people deeply personal things, she found this incredibly easy to say. 'I financed it from the start.'

Max nodded slowly and his face opened up in acknowledgement. 'I'm not surprised.'

She was. He used to give her hell about being well off and having it easy. This showed that the awkward areas of their past were wrapped up and not to be aired again. Unless they were to get close enough to slip between the sheets one day, then the airing would be all about the few amazing times they had shared. 'Thank you. Not many people know and I'd prefer it stays that way.'

'I won't be racing off to tell all and sundry,' he assured her.

'Good.' She believed him. Her head felt lighter and she was smiling. Max wasn't the devil she recalled. Had he ever been? Or had she been so focused on keeping him at arm's length she'd been totally wrong about him? But she wasn't good at reading men. Damned hopeless, actually.

Pulling her arm free, she shoved her hands in her jeans pockets and strolled into the building, pretending nonchalance every step of the way.

CHAPTER FOUR

WHAT MORE DO I really want out of life? Lily wondered as she sat before the fire in her lounge later that night. Love. Yes. A child. Yes. Once she'd settled into the Remuera Medical Hub and had created a place amongst other focused medical practitioners she'd follow through on that.

She wanted family, badly. Children were essential to life. Growing up ensconced with loving parents and brothers who gave so much to each other had taught her lots about living and caring. When she and Leo had got engaged, she'd naturally thought he'd want the same. He adored his family, yet when he left he'd said she'd misunderstood, that he wasn't ready to be a father, might never be. Had she ever understood him? Breaking up had hurt, yet her biggest regret was the lost opportunity to have children. Had she done Leo a disservice by accepting his love when it was now obvious she hadn't loved him enough?

A phone ringing cut through the quiet of the house. Max? Why would it be? He wasn't a friend to call for the sake of it. Digging around the armchair cushion, her fingers wrapped around the phone. 'Charlotte, how's things?'

Her friend laughed. 'Nothing out of the usual, I'm afraid. All rather boring really.'

'So you rang me for some entertainment?' Lily's attempt to laugh fell flat.

'I want to hear all about Dr Bryant. I presume you've seen him at the camp.'

In the background Lily could hear Charlotte pouring liquid. 'Wine or tea?' What was she going to say? She usually told her closest friend everything, but… But what? It wasn't as though she had anything to hide.

'Tea. Come on, spill.'

Lily drew a breath. 'I told him my role in the camp.'

'Knew I should've poured a wine.' Then, 'Why? I set up the trust in a way it would be very hard for anyone to find out and you tell the one man sure to give you a hard time, and maybe let it slip to others? As your lawyer I'm saying that was not your brightest move, Lily.'

'And as my friend?' Had she been testing Max to see if he had changed as much as she was beginning to suspect? If so, she'd chosen the wrong subject for that. Lily waited.

'What did he say?' Charlotte asked.

'He wasn't surprised and won't tell others. I believe him on both counts.' He had sounded genuine. 'Max is not the man I once worked with. He doesn't appear to be looking for ways to prove he's better than anyone else, for one.'

'What about the man you slept with?'

No idea. 'No getting away from our past. Anyway, let's drop this. I can't undo what I said, and frankly I doubt there's any need. I feel I can trust Max.' It was in the way he listened to her without rolling his eyes, as if to say, 'Yeah, right', in his ready acceptance of her for who she was now. Not that he knew much about what had gone on over the past years, but that's why she felt he had become a more trustworthy man.

'There's another way of looking at this. Someone, one day, is bound to find out you funded setting up the camp. These things happen, though we have got this one pretty tight. But we're not the only people who know and a slip of the tongue is all it takes.'

Lily pictured her grandmother lying in her hospital bed, smiling as Lily outlined what she wanted to do with her share of her inheritance. In a way it had been an uncomfortable moment as it had underlined what lay ahead for Granny. The pneumonia had taken hold and it had only been a matter of time. Lily had spent many hours at her bedside when work hadn't been taking up her time. Telling Max had reminded her of that day, and the sense of doing the right thing that had gripped her and become a passion that never let up.

'I was clearing the air between us, laying the past to rest. We're going to be working together, and I want a clean slate.'

She also wanted to learn more about him. Like what had happened to his determination to be a top-notch surgeon? What had caused those dark shadows to fill his eyes in the middle of a conversation? Whenever she saw them an urge overtook her to hug him, tell him he'd be fine.

Charlotte broke into her meanderings. 'So, tell, is Max still as good looking as he used to be?'

Lily grinned. 'No. He's better. A hunk, in an older, more subdued way, like he's finally comfortable in his own body. There're shiny silvery grey streaks in his hair, which he doesn't hide, more like wears them as a badge for something he's dealt with.' Charlotte would be loving this. 'He doesn't rush in to be the hero when someone's in need of a doctor. We had an incident this morning when my neighbour had a stroke, and we worked well together.'

'Whoa. Am I really hearing this?' Charlotte teased. 'Seems you're starting to like him. Your voice softens when you say his name. You sure you aren't in the market for a romance?'

'Very certain.' Lily crossed her fingers. Had she just lied? Max was changing her mind about a few things. 'Becoming friends is one thing, falling for him something else.' But unwittingly he had ticked the sincere and kind boxes she needed filled if she were ever to take another chance on romance. What was she thinking? Sure, she wanted to find love, but equally she wasn't going to risk being hurt again.

'She protests too much, methinks,' Charlotte said quietly. 'Be careful, Lily. You might be over Leo, but you're still vulnerable. I know you've got the position you want, and would love nothing more than to be a mother, but take your time, especially over Max.'

It felt good knowing Charlotte had her back. 'Thanks for being there and understanding.'

'As if you don't return the favour,' Charlotte said before hanging up.

Lily unwound herself from the chair and went in search of a can of soup. If only she'd hooked up with a man who understood her and accepted her for who she was, instead of the two she'd known, she might not be on a solo path for a family. An image of Max filled her mind, his eyes sad and body slumped. The new Max, the one she couldn't help but like already.

They'd talked about having kids. Did he want the same things? Was he looking for love? Had he changed so much he no longer did the short flings and walk-away routine? Wait. She sucked a short, sharp breath. Had Max been in love and had his heart broken? It stood to reason that might have happened. Despite his previous playboy rep, if Max had fallen for a woman, it would've been with one hundred percent focus.

The sort of love she'd twice thought she'd found, and given. Only now she understood she hadn't loved either man anywhere nearly as much as she'd believed. Or she had, and now wanted something deeper and stronger, a love that knew no boundaries and didn't falter at the first hurdle.

Only since coming in contact with Max again had this realisation dawned.

She had loved both men, in turn, and hadn't been enough to keep either of them. She might not be the right person to get married and live happily ever after. No, she would not accept that. She *was* loving, cared deeply for the people important to her, and would do anything to make them happy.

As she fully intended to do for her child should she have one.

A text landed in her phone.

Hi, Auntie Lily. I had a great day. Loves ya, J.

Lily's heart melted.

Loves you too. See you tomorrow. xxx

She wasn't expected to turn up at the camp daily, but she'd go and see Josie.

And Max.

'Catch, Auntie Lily.'

Lily spun around, scanning the space between her and where Josie's shout had come from, and saw an object hurtling towards her. Snatching the basketball out of the air, she hurled it to the boy on the same side of the net as Josie.

A whistle blew. 'Foul.' Max grinned. 'Intervention from the sideline.'

'Yes,' shouted the teens on the opposing side, and one ducked underneath to retrieve the ball rolling their way.

'Spoilsport.' Lily laughed.

Max shook his head, grinning happily. 'You think I want to be nailed to the ground and have this lot riding over me in their wheelchairs?'

'Now, there's an idea,' she retorted. 'What's the score?'

'Five all.'

'Right, come on, guys. Let's whip their backsides,' she called to Josie and her partner.

Josie fist pumped. 'Yeah, let's.'

Max nodded to the other team. 'Come on, give it to them, you two.'

Lily watched the girl balance on her prosthetic leg and swing her fist at the ball. The bravery these children showed melted her heart. Their strength was almost inherent. Her hand rested on her stomach briefly. Children were amazing. Her gaze slipped sideways. Max was engrossed in the game, giving himself over to the kids. *Father material.* Absolutely, but for her child? Unlikely. They were getting on fine but it would be a huge leap, one she was not ready for by any stretch of the imagination. So why did the idea keep popping up?

'Yippee,' Josie yelled. 'Six to us.'

Kids on the sidelines shouted enthusiastically.

'Time to change ends,' Max called.

Lily handed the players water bottles to guzzle from before they started the second half of the match. 'You want one?' She held out a bottle to Max.

'This is hot work.' He laughed, taking the bottle, his fingers brushing hers sending sparks up her arm.

Quickly pulling back, she said, 'You're enjoying it.' Why had she moved away? The tingling in her hand made her feel more alive.

Max fixed his gaze on her mouth as he placed the bottle between his lips and poured water down his throat. Desire filled his eyes.

Tightness clamped her chest. Snatching up the last bottle, she tried to swallow some liquid but her throat was closed. Great. Right in the middle of a conversation she'd gone and lost the gist of what they'd been discussing. Glancing around, she saw children everywhere. Of course. The kids. That's what today, the week, was about. Not Max and herself. But it was ridiculously easy to be sidetracked by those beautiful khaki eyes filled with desire for *her*.

Max seemed to be having similar difficulty remembering where they were. He spun away, staring towards the sea. When he finally spoke, his voice was rough. 'They're all so keen to win and to have a good time while they're at it.' He was onto it. The kids.

'Keener than they'll be when it's time to sit in the classroom and discuss plans for their futures.' Keep talking sensibly and surely the need would die down?

'Some are a little young to be worrying about that yet,' Max noted, still facing away.

'The psychologists don't agree. Something about being prepared so they can handle setbacks more easily.' This *was* getting easier by the word, but she needed to talk non-stop for ten minutes to be totally heat free.

'What does Josie want to become?'

'A beautician.' Lily saw her niece hobbling to the end of the court. Keep talking, move on. 'It might be a passing fad. She's just discovered make-up in a big way.'

'I noticed the heavy mascara. Right, time to get the game underway again.'

Lily sat on a park bench, watching Max dashing up and down the edge of the sand court, blowing his whistle, shouting encouragement. He was in his element with these teenagers giving their mates cheek, his face was again clear and open, his eyes sparkling with enjoyment.

'Hello, Doctor.' Michelle stood beside her, balancing on crutches. 'What an awesome place.'

'Isn't it? When did you get here?'

'Nearly an hour ago. I've been talking to Logan. He says there's a shortage of beds so even if I chose to stay on I can't.'

'I'll find you somewhere. Don't worry about it.' There were empty bedrooms at the beach house. 'What do you think of the set-up so far?'

'It's amazing. From the main building I saw some boys playing soccer and their sheer determination to score is mind-blowing. I wanted to rush out and join them, help the guy coaching them.'

'Why didn't you? That's the idea of you being here,' Lily told her.

'I was with Logan, getting the rundown on the camp.' Michelle's cheeks were turning pink.

Lily shook her head. Logan and Michelle? Why not? A blinding thought struck. Was romance in the air out here in Whangaparaoa? Did that mean others were going to feel the love this week? Josie and her friend? Her and Max? Lily leapt to her feet. No way. Never. Her gaze went immediately to him as he blew the final whistle. She would not be hurt again. She did want love, but doubted she had the courage to risk her heart once more. Not even with Max.

Look at him. His face had matured to heart-stopping attractiveness. His mouth was kind and soft, and she already knew from the past the sensations those lips created on her feverish skin. Skin that right this moment was prickling. His curls made her fingers restless and her lungs squeeze painfully. Spinning around before he looked over and caught her out, she breathed deep for composure, which wasn't coming. He'd been a wonderful lover. Quivering was going on in her legs. Her head felt light. She swore. She might be in trouble here.

'Hi, Max,' Michelle called across the space, and hobbled across to the courtside.

'You made it. Not that I thought you wouldn't,' he added hurriedly.

'I was up and ready at five this morning. Now I've got something else to focus on other than myself, I want to get cracking.'

Lily dragged her feet over to join them. 'What did Logan suggest you do?'

'Join in the activities.' Michelle waved a crutch between them.

Max laughed. 'You'll go down a treat.' He raised one eyebrow in Lily's direction. 'But we already knew that.'

'We did.' It was still hard to talk sensibly while trying to move past the desire Max evoked in her, but she kept trying. Easier if she focused on Michelle and not Max. 'Not all these guys want to be anything great; most only want to be accepted for who they are.'

'I always feel on the fringe with my friends because I'm driven to get ahead.'

'How long do you think you'll stay?' Max asked Michelle.

'There's the problem. The accommodation is chock full. Lily says she'll sort it, though, so who knows?'

'You can stay at my family's house along the road,' Lily told her.

'Thanks. I'd prefer to be here on the spot so I can chat to anyone any time, but your house is better than heading back to the city,' Michelle said, then shook her head. 'There I go again. Sorry. It was a generous offer and I'm happy to accept.'

Lily managed a brief laugh. 'Don't worry. I like your honesty.'

'If it means a difference in how long you remain at the camp you can have my room, Michelle. I'll bunk down somewhere else.' Max's eyes were on Lily as he said that.

Leaving her with only one thing to say, though it came out slowly and warily. 'You can move into the beach house if you'd like.' Max in the house for meals and showers, and sleeping? Hell, she couldn't remain uninterested when there was a kilometre between them. It would be impossible to remain neutral with him staying between the same four walls as her.

'Talk to you later if there's nowhere else.' Was he saying he wasn't interested in sharing her house? When he'd offered to swap with Michelle? She couldn't blame him for having second thoughts.

'No problem. I'm going to find Josie for a chat.' Not about boys and condoms or being safe, tempting as that was. Though she would keep an eye on the relationship between her niece and the boy who put all that colour in her face and excitement in her eyes. Blimey, was that how *she* looked whenever she thought about Max? Hadn't she just got into a pickle over him? Yes, and still felt at odds with herself. As soon as she'd talked with Josie, she'd head to the house and pull on her running gear. Action was required to quieten the brain.

'Auntie Lily, who's that lady on the crutches?'

'Michelle Baxter. She plays—'

'Netball for the North Shore. She's awesome.' Josie squealed and charged across to her apparent idol. 'Hi, Michelle, I'm Josie. I watch most of your games. You're great.'

Michelle laughed, and said, 'Thanks for that.'

'What have you done to your leg? Is it serious?' Josie didn't stop to think how her questions might be received, but that might be good for Michelle. It was how strangers often treated Josie. But still…

'Some delinquent shoved me out of a bus I was boarding and my ankle's broken. It's lucky my wrist wasn't broken after all.'

'But you're going to England soon.'

Michelle's smile slipped. 'I was.'

About to step in and shut her niece down, Lily opened her mouth but Michelle cut her off. 'It's hugely disappointing, but I'm getting used to the thought of staying behind. It's a block in my

career, but not the end. Tell me, what's your favourite sport? I saw you playing netball earlier.'

Lily hesitated, watching Josie talk about how
she liked wheelchair basketball the best, and any
game that involved using her arms more than
her legs were fun.

'They're getting along fine,' Max said quietly beside her.

Her skin prickled. 'They're reacting to each
other as I'd hoped they would, only I hadn't spe-
cifically factored Josie into the picture.'

'Why would you? It was chance that Josie's
the first person to waylay Michelle.' Max
sounded thoughtful. 'Seems you might've nailed
it. They're both animated and talking non-stop
about the situations they're in. Let's leave them
to it and grab a coffee and sandwich before the
hordes devour all the food I saw being prepared
earlier.'

Lily all but bounced up the lawn, wearing a
wide smile and humming under her breath.

'So would it be all right if I did doss down at
your house?'

Okay, maybe she should quieten the happiness level. But it *would* be good to have him
closer on and off; as long as she controlled her
hormones and kept her heart from racing and
her skin from prickling. 'Wouldn't have offered

if it wasn't.' Would she? Was she playing dangerously now?

Stop, Lily. Think this through. You could get hurt again.

Max grinned. 'Think I might be lucky enough to get a meal at your place?'

Too late to stop this. The whole thing was expanding rapidly. First a bed, now meals. What next? Don't go there. 'You haven't asked if I know how to cook.' She wanted to clap her hands in the air and laugh. Max was going to stay with her.

Max turned around. 'Hey, Josie, can your aunt cook a mean dinner?'

Josie's eyes widened with a hint of something Lily was afraid to interpret. 'Ask her to make beef bourguignon. It's to die for.'

Little wretch. No denying the cheeky smile or the 'I've got you back for all those times you've teased me' gleam in Josie's eyes. 'Haven't you got something better to do than harass your favourite aunt?'

'Nope.'

'Imp.' Lily aimed for the main building.

Max strolled along beside her. 'After I've finished here I'll drive to the nearest shops to get some wine to go with that beef.'

'Guess that means I am making the casserole.' Her mind was going through the fridge for mushrooms and beef stock. 'Luckily there's beef in the freezer.'

'Text if there's anything you need. I won't head away before five.'

'Will do.' Outside the building, she paused, not sure what to say but feeling there was something she needed to get out.

'Relax, Lily. I appreciate the offer of a room. I won't make a pest of myself. I'll be here most of the time anyway.' Max touched her lightly on the shoulder, sending sparks right to the tips of her toes. 'We're good. We haven't argued, and I doubt we will, other than over the occasional differences that occur at the medical hub.'

At the same time as wishing he didn't sound so serious, his touch did a number on her libido. Obviously it meant nothing to him. There was a message there she should abide by. So she should forget the disappointment sliding through her, act normal. 'You think?' Normal?

His eyes widened. 'I do.' Then doubt crept in, bringing the dark shade into that serious look as he stepped back. 'Don't tell me I'm wrong. I don't want to return to the way things were between us.' That elusive sadness filtered through his gaze before disappearing. 'I learned a lot from that time because of you and I hope I've matured and understand people better. You as well.'

What had happened to him? That was a huge admission, and totally out of left field. The more she saw the more she believed something big had occurred, such as a broken heart. They were both like flotsam floating through life, hiding their hurts, in her case aiming for happiness from a new and different perspective from her previous attempts.

What was Max hoping for? Planning on achieving? Who did he wish to spend his life with? She wasn't about to find out while standing here outside the building filling up with hungry teenagers wanting food. It was doubtful she'd ever learn what was behind that sadness. But he had said he'd matured partly because of her, so anything was possible. She gave him a smile. 'Let's grab lunch.' She had a beef bourguignon to prepare, and it was going to be her best effort ever.

Her smile slipped and she stopped. Less than a week ago she had been struggling with the idea of working with Max. Now he was coming to stay in her family home. What was she doing? Romance wasn't on the cards. Max definitely wasn't either. He might be different but how different?

CHAPTER FIVE

SO THIS WAS what married life might be like, Max thought. Easy, caring, sharing. Nothing like his parents' relationship even before their bitter divorce. 'Sit down and take a load off,' he instructed Lily after a scrumptious dinner. Another string to her bow. 'Want a hot drink?'

'A hot chocolate wouldn't go amiss.' Lily glanced at him with a cheeky smile. 'I've got a really sweet tooth, which is why I run.'

As if she was overweight. She looked more gorgeous than ever now her curves had filled out a little. 'Not to keep fit, then?' He laughed, trying to ignore the picture filling his head of Lily sprawled across his bed one night a long time ago. She'd been beautiful, and now she was even more so from what little he could see.

'That'd be crazy. The chocolate mix is on the baking shelf in the pantry.'

'You can find it blindfolded?' Having lighthearted fun with Lily was a new concept, and one he liked.

'Naturally.' Her chair balanced on its back legs as she watched him make their drinks.

Yes, he'd join her with hot chocolate. Anything was better than going to bed alone and dreaming about what might be if he let go his determination to remain single. That determination could be his undoing—or give him something precious. As had happened with medicine. At first he'd been resolute in showing his father how he loved him and wanted the same in return, but what had happened was far better. Medicine was him, and he got so much more from it than he gave. He'd also finally won quiet approval from his father, acknowledged during the cancer battle. What might happen if he could dispel this painful need to remain single?

He might hurt someone else. That's what.

Lily was chattering on, thankfully blind to his pain. 'I started running in Singapore as a way of getting out and about without looking like a lost tourist. I liked getting away from being behind four walls all the time. Usually I followed the smell of street food and cancelled the plus side of running before returning to our apartment.'

He stood straighter, sucked in his gut. 'Our apartment? You weren't on your own?' From what he'd heard when she'd been appointed to the medical hub, she was now.

'I lived with my fiancé, Leo. We met at the medical centre when I moved to Singapore.'

Lived with. In the past? How far could he go with his curiosity? Why this driving need to know?

Because I like Lily a lot. Possibly more than like.

'It didn't work out?'

Lily's smile flattened, her face closed. 'Not after a while. I came home from work one night to find him all packed up, waiting to tell me he was heading home to Scotland and a woman from his past he'd been in contact with for a few months.'

'I'm sorry to hear that.' She'd been getting over another failed relationship when they'd had their fling. At first he'd wondered if he'd been mad, asking her to his home, but she hadn't brought baggage, and had seemed instead to be happy to spend time with him. It had been beyond wonderful as he had begun to see Lily differently from the woman he'd worked with. Until the morning she'd got up and said that was the end. Talk about a sharp slap in the face. And a dent to his ego. Most of all, he'd felt he'd lost an opportunity for elusive happiness, which had only made him go even harder in locking down his dreams of love.

'You deserve better than that.'

'I do.' She nodded. 'It's behind me and I'm not in a hurry for another relationship.'

It sounded like a warning. About what? But at least he knew. They were on similar pages regarding relationships, though for different reasons. He should be relieved, but instead his stomach sank and his heart was heavy.

Placing a steaming mug in front of her, Max sat opposite, his hands wrapped around his mug. 'I've never been in a long-term relationship.' He gulped. Lily's truthfulness had started him talking. It was long overdue, and not as difficult as he'd have believed.

Surprise lifted her face, widened her eyes. 'I got that wrong,' she said. 'I thought maybe you'd had your heart crushed and that's why you...' She paused. 'Why you stuck to nothing more involved than flings.'

'When I was training I didn't want to get too intense with someone and find myself distracted from achieving my medical degree.'

'You were that determined you gave up other important things to achieve it?'

'I did. My father never had the opportunity to follow his dreams, so I felt driven to make mine come true. It was also a way to show my mother she was wrong to leave me and take my sister with her when she left Dad.' Talk about laying his heart on the line. Now she knew more about him than any woman he'd spent time with. He should be heading down the hall to the bedroom to get away—there was a first, getting away from any woman to go to a bedroom.

He sighed. A load had lifted from his chest by telling her what lay behind his modus operandi. And to Lily, strange as it was. Or was it? When she'd been the first woman to ever have him yearning for something more, deeper, than his usual short interactions, this felt right.

'Your parents were separated?' Sadness blinked out of those soft eyes.

'When I was ten. Mum felt I'd be better off raised by Dad, and not have her and my sister fluffing over me.' It had always felt like an excuse. No one had asked him what he might want. 'Mum didn't move far so I visited often.'

'But it wasn't the same.'

'Visiting your parent? Not at all.'

Her hand covered his for a warm moment then she gave him a break, trying to lighten the mood. 'I was so lucky with my family. Growing up on the farm with my brothers, I was always out to prove I was as good if not better than them at getting into mischief or doing jobs around the place. There was no such thing as too heavy or too hard. I could do it.' Her smile was wistful.

'It was a wonderful childhood, and stood me in good stead to get through med school. Though there were times I thought I'd taken on more than I could manage, I never let anyone know.'

He'd seen that. 'Not once in those two years in ED did I think you were struggling. Or had you found your strengths by then?' He couldn't quite believe this conversation with the woman he'd once believed more interested in herself than anyone else. Because she had left him, which was not the usual way flings went with him.

She was strong, tough, but there was a softness to her he'd not seen back then. Because he hadn't wanted to? In case he felt too much for her? Or had he been so intent on getting through what he'd set out to do medically that he hadn't stopped to really see Lily for who she was? What opportunities had he lost? Did he want to try to retrieve them? Or continue on this lonely journey to be safe? His stomach tightened painfully.

Lily cut through his dour thoughts. 'My family's wonderful. We're all close. If I could have I'd have taken up farming too, but it was the one thing my father was adamant I wouldn't do. My dad kept reiterating how I wanted to be a doctor, had done since I was a teenager. He told me it was important to follow my heart and not go into farming to prove to my brothers I could do it as well as them.' She sipped her hot chocolate. 'He had a point. There was a lot of that proving myself again and again in my need to stay on the land.'

'Have you ever regretted your choice?'

'Not once. My dad knows me well.'

'You're lucky.' His father still hurt over his wife leaving him. And for him there hadn't been a lot of sharing dreams and goals or fun times over a beer or going fishing together. He'd always wondered what he'd done wrong to be kept at a distance, but after the cancer he'd come to see that was how his dad coped with everything. But then he could say he owed his father because that's what had made him want to prove he could be worthy of being loved and believed in. Hence the reason he'd become a doctor. What about a husband? A father?

Damn you, Lily. You're causing havoc with my thinking.

'I know. Which is why I've stood by him at the awards ceremonies. The only reason, in fact.' She grinned, obviously unaware of the effect she was having on him. Her striking face became childlike with that grin splitting her mouth wide and her wide eyes glittering like diamonds in the sun.

'Is it too late to apologise for being a prat?' He grinned back, his heart pounding and his toes curling. Being so at ease with her was strange and wonderful all at once. 'I'm serious. I wasn't kind to you back then.'

'If we start apologising we'll be busy all evening, and I can think of better ways to spend the time.'

So can I. The chocolate went down the wrong way, causing him to cough. Quickly on his feet before Lily could pat his back and send his heart rate into dangerous territory, he moved away to take long, slow breaths. And swallow his rising disappointment over not being able to follow up on the longing gripping him. They were not repeating that fling. Not for anything.

He doubted he'd be able to get over it as easily as last time, and there'd been a little hitch then where he'd regretted it, so he was not getting involved with Lily. She was a colleague at the medical centre. She might want a casual relationship after her last one had gone wrong, but he already knew that wasn't all he wanted, and getting into a serious relationship was a no-no.

A warm hand did touch his shoulder, sending heat through his tense muscles. 'You all right?'

'Yes.'

The hand retracted instantly. 'Right.' Lily walked away.

The air cooled but not his body. *Come back. I'll explain.* No. He wouldn't. He wasn't ready. Would he ever be? Could he consider a real relationship with her? Look forward and not let the past darken his thinking? If only he could manage that. Twelve months ago he'd begun moving on a little, had started looking ahead to a bright, happy future. Then he'd had a scare and thought the cancer had returned. That had set him back, strengthened his resolve not to hurt anyone.

Now here was Lily, and he'd started looking forward with a fierce longing that grew every day. Was he being a fool to let the past dictate his future? He could live till he was eighty and regret not marrying and having a family. Or, glancing at Lily's retreating back, he could grab the chance for happiness and run with it. Take the setbacks on the chin, like he'd done with most things all his life before this.

Lily opened her laptop and drank the last of the lukewarm chocolate while waiting for the page to come up. Max had told her more about himself than ever before. They were mostly relaxed in each other's company.

'Max, have you kept in touch with any of the staff we worked with in Auckland ED?'

'We've all mostly lost touch.' He was staring at his feet as he talked. 'Everyone got involved in specialist training and then starting to build their careers, having families, buying homes.'

'You've bought a property in Auckland? Got anyone living with you?'

'I'm on my own, living in a rundown three-bed house I bought in a cul-de-sac along the road from the medical hub, and that's going to keep me busy and happy for years to come. It's enough.'

Something wasn't ringing true but she couldn't put her finger on what it might be. Was he happy? Busy? Was there anyone else in his life? She wasn't prepared to ask more about that. 'What about the sports side of your work? Does it take you to many matches? Rugby? Cricket? League?'

'All of the above. I did a day at the international tennis tournament in January. Most weekends I attend at least one game of some sort, though now I'm officially the team doctor for one of the North Shore franchises I have less time for other games. Which means not a lot is getting done on the house, but…' he shrugged '…it doesn't matter. I'll get there someday.'

Her phone rang. 'It's Josie. Hey, bright spark. What's up?'

'I've been talking with Ollie about his family and stuff. Lily, he's cool. I like him more than last time we were here.'

What was she supposed to say to that?

'He wants me to visit his house and go to the movies with him next week.'

Did kids still do that? 'What's wrong with watching a movie on TV?'

'His parents and sister would be there.'

I get it. You can't hold hands and snog.

'This is something you'll have to sort out with Mum and Dad.' She was passing the buck. Her role didn't include setting the dating rules for a demanding fourteen-year-old.

'They'll like Ollie so it'll be okay.' Josie talked on, barely taking a breath.

Lily sat listening, smiling at her niece's exuberance for life. It was wonderful considering the setbacks she'd had over the years because of the spina bifida and people who couldn't accept she had the same aspirations as everyone else.

'You've got to meet him, Lily. You'll like him. Everyone does. He's so cute.'

Lily tried not to laugh. Had she been like this at fourteen? At fifteen there'd been that boy, Jeff, who'd kissed her at the school disco and she'd thought it was revolting. But then there'd

been Johnny and his kisses had shown Jeff to
be an amateur. She watched Max reading mes-
sages on his phone and smiled. He just did that
to her. Made her feel good. Which was unexpected. Or was it? She'd been quick to offer him
somewhere to stay. And equally fast to rue the
invitation in case she couldn't cope with him in
her space. Yet now he was here she was happy
spending time with him. Maybe she could take
another chance.

Slow down, Lily.

'Auntie, are you listening?'

'Sure. I'll come along during the day to watch
your game.' *Concentrate.*

After minutes more of Josie telling her how
wonderful Ollie was, Lily finally managed to
put her phone down. Dropping her head into
her hands, she groaned. 'Josie thinks she's falling in love. At fourteen. Blimey. I need to tell
my brother.'

'No, you don't,' Max growled. 'She'd never
talk to you again.'

'True. I can't do that. I'm her trusted go-to
adult when she has a fall-out with her parents.
But love, at her age.'

'Are you saying you didn't think some
knobbly-kneed guy in grey school shorts was
to die for when you were that old?'

'Johnny Barstow. He had muscular legs, good

knees, and the start of whiskers on his chin.'
She began laughing.

'Cassey Jones, long blonde hair and skinny,'
Max recounted. 'She danced like a crazed person. Had all the guys lining up for a kiss.' He
filled a glass with water. 'Here.'

She hiccupped and took the glass, her fingers
brushing his. 'Thanks. This is the closest I've
been to parenting, and I'm lucky it's funny. My
brother and sister-in-law aren't going to think
so.' Neither would she when her turn came.

'Are they very strict?' Max sat opposite her.

'More likely they'll remember themselves at
high school. They met when they were sixteen
and haven't been apart since.' She downed the
water. 'Still get on brilliantly.'

'What about your other brother? He married?'

'Yes, finally. His wife's Italian and they kept
seesawing between which country they'd live
in if they'd actually tie the knot or stay in their
respective places, if he'd give up farming when
it was so important to him, if she'd give up the
family bakery when there was no one else to
take over.' Lily adored Aurora and could sympathise with the decisions she and Toby had
had to make.

'Your brother would've given up his share of
the farm for her?'

'I believe so. But Aurora understood he'd

have struggled living in Florence, and while it wasn't easy to leave her family she has, and to her full credit she's making a real go of being a Kiwi farmer's wife. Her family visit often. There's a baby on the way, too.'

'True love by the sound of it.' Max was looking at her with a smile. 'They're lucky.'

'More than most people I know.'

What about you, Max? Has anyone tempted the heart inside that sexy chest?

What about children? That question kept popping up like she really needed to know.

Max's phone pinged and she left him to it, occasionally glancing across while she did some work for the camp online.

Around ten, Lily yawned and stood up to stretch. 'Think I'll hit the sack.' It was early for her, but her arms and shoulders still ached from the chainsawing effort yesterday. Tomorrow she'd finish stacking the wood that didn't need to be split. 'See you in the morning.'

Max watched her as she stretched, making even more muscles tight. 'Don't get up for me. I can fix my own breakfast.' He stood.

'I don't lie in.'

'See you then.' He waited for her to move past him.

Lily hesitated and lifted her gaze to meet his.

'Never thought I'd say this, but I'm enjoying spending time with you.' Ouch, she shouldn't have said it quite like that. 'I mean...'

'Relax. I know what you meant. It's okay.' His finger under her chin was warm and gentle.

When she looked deeper into his eyes a thrill rolled down her spine. She leaned closer at the same time he did. 'Max,' she whispered.

His mouth was close to hers, his eyes open, watching her. 'Ah, Lily.'

Neither moved, stuck in a warm moment. Move forward and everything changed. Pull back and... She had no idea. What did she want? Right this moment she craved his kiss. Every nerve ending was crying out to be touched, to be woken up in a way she hadn't known since last time they'd been together. Wanting to find love didn't mean getting involved with Max. She stepped back.

Max reached for her hand, raised it to his lips to place a delicate kiss on her palm. 'Goodnight, Lily.' His gruff voice sent tingles of need and heat and happiness spreading through her.

That one step forward would bring her body up to his and the possibility of satisfying this continuous and growing longing he triggered in her. Pulling her hand away, she watched to see if he was upset with her for breaking contact. He didn't appear to be, but neither did he look relieved. Was he in the same messed-up head space she was? She wasn't waiting to find out. She might need him, but she wasn't prepared to accept she might take another chance at love. 'See you tomorrow.'

Charging towards her bedroom, she resisted the urge to turn around and see if he was watching her flight. Damn, damn, damn. She'd just made a mistake. Backing off had been the right thing to do, but being in that situation in the first place had been wrong. It only proved she hadn't quite convinced herself she wasn't going to get close to a man again. Not that she had to avoid the occasional fling to prevent going crazy with unrequited lust. But Max was not the man for that. Sure, he'd fix the lust, while removing the handbrake she'd hauled on to her future.

Closing her door with a thud, she leaned back against it to stare up at the ceiling. He was a great lover, but didn't want a permanent relationship. Or so she'd surmised from the fact he'd never had one. She wouldn't repeat her mistakes but hell. What to do about that sense of something more than sex and attraction that had worried her during their fling and was gnawing away now?

He hadn't laughed at her or said she was a tease. He'd been considerate when she'd backed away just now. And disappointed.

As disappointed as the thudding behind her ribs acknowledged she was.

Lily slid down the door and pulled her knees up to her chin, wound her arms around them and closed her eyes. Max had always managed to disrupt her equilibrium one way or another. Now, when she'd decided to focus on her career and hopefully becoming a mother, he had her wondering if taking another chance on love might be worth it.

Missing pieces to her puzzle were beginning to fall into place in her heart. He understood her, knew her better for their past and wasn't running away. She hadn't told him her dream yet, and that could squash any feelings he might have for her. If any. She sighed. This was probably all wishful thinking.

The sand was hard after the overnight downpour. Max's knees took a pounding as he ran along the beach, but the discomfort was worth it just to be able to breathe fresh air and clear the cobwebs from his head. It had been a restless night, evidenced by the bed cover on the floor and the sheets in a bundle around his legs when he'd woken from what little sleep he'd got. Every time he'd closed his eyes Lily had been there, her face filling his mind, allowing nothing else in. Every breath gave him a repeat of her citrus scent, making his palms tingle and his skin tighten. And more.

By being herself, she'd got to him. In a way no other woman had. She didn't try to flatter him or fawn over him. She accepted him for who he was, or for who he showed he was. It was almost possible to imagine a relationship without instantly bringing up the shutters.

Standing with her, not kissing those full lips, not wrapping his arms around her to pull her length against him, had taken all the self-control he had and then some. He'd wanted her. Badly. His resolve not to touch her would have failed if she hadn't pulled back when she had. Even then he'd wanted to touch her, take her in his arms, and ignore the fact she'd stopped moving towards him. The need hadn't died down in her eyes. She'd found it no easier to walk away than him.

Which made it harder to keep his distance. Two more nights staying in her house was going to turn him into an overheated zombie. He was already tired from lack of sleep. But if he swapped with someone else at the camp Lily mightn't talk to him again. Or she might be relieved.

'Can I run with you?'

Max glanced sideways to the enquiring look

coming from the lad who'd caught up to him. 'Certainly.'

They fell into a rhythm and continued down the beach, getting further away from the camp. Max was impressed. The young man had a club foot yet wasn't showing any signs of difficulty or discomfort.

'You're Dr Max, aren't you? I'm Ollie.'

Max nodded. 'You played basketball yesterday.' Josie had been at the court, screaming encouragement at him.

'You know Josie's aunt, don't you?'

'We worked together a few years back, and are about to do so again.' He sensed the lad wanted more than that. 'I'm staying at her family's beach house this week.'

'I really like Josie a lot, and hope her aunt will be okay with us spending time together.'

'I can't see why not.' It depended what they did in that time, Max mused. Not that it was his place to say so. 'Have you met Lily?'

'Josie's going to introduce us today. I want her to like me or Josie might tell me to get lost.'

They'd reached the end of the beach and Max stopped, took some deep breaths and gazed across the bumpy sea. 'From what I've seen, you don't know Josie very well if you believe that.'

Ollie grinned. 'That's what I thought. Thanks for talking to me, Dr Max. It's cool.'

Everyone needed to talk about personal things sometimes, and he was available for these kids this week. 'No problem.' Not that he'd helped solve anything but sometimes all it took was to be a good listener. If only he could download all the stuff in his head as easily. 'Let's go back for a shower and some breakfast.'

He had to get over this. As much as Lily attracted him, keeping his feet on the ground was imperative for his sanity. She had him talking when he never told people his deepest thoughts. It made him feel connected to her in ways he'd not known before. It went beyond the monumental physical attraction to places he wasn't used to sharing. His ribs ached from the continuous pounding going on. Lily was special, and he was afraid. He could hurt them both if he gave in to this yearning for love. They must not have another fling. She'd had two failed relationships. He wasn't adding to the list.

His pace picked up. His arms pumped, his head pushed forward, as he drove his body to work as hard as possible, trying to outrun the desire filling him, the longing for a normal, happy relationship. With Lily? Yes, damn it, with Lily. He stumbled, righted himself, and continued at the breakneck pace. These feelings slam dunked him again and again. The sense that they could have had more before had bloomed into a roaring awareness of everything about her. The vulnerability he'd felt back then had returned. Larger, more frightening. Had he got more to lose now?

Had he been trying too hard to remain single? But he had to. The five-year clearance from the oncologist was two years away. And when…if he did… No, damn it, when. No more negativity. His results had been all he could want so far. Constantly waiting for the axe to fall was wasting the opportunity to be happy. Okay, so when he got the final all-clear, he still wasn't going to marry and have children. But he could have some fun. If he kept his heart out of the picture.

The path leading up to the camp buildings veered to the left. Max stopped and leaned over, hands on hips, his lungs burning as he dragged in air. So much for a cruisy run to wake himself up. He had been awake all right, just not in cruise mode. Lily Scott had got to him once more. It might not be as the result of a massive argument, or calling off their sexy nights, but her generosity, her smiles, her honesty were even more potent. Far more dangerous. Because he wanted her. All of her. And he couldn't have her. It wouldn't be fair. An expletive tore out of him.

'You okay, Doctor?' Ollie ran up the path, looking in a lot better shape than Max was.

'Fine,' Max croaked through a breath. Fine and dandy.

'See you later.' And the kid was off, making like there was nothing wrong with his foot. Which there wasn't with his great attitude and determination.

'Something I could learn from,' Max conceded. 'Thought I was meant to be helping these guys, not the other way round.'

Resilience was the catchword for the camp. Physical resilience. Peer pressure resilience. Mental fortitude to face what other people threw at them. All these teens seemed to have bags of it and yet there were times each and every one of them suffered doubts or hurt.

Straightening up, Max started walking up the path. He liked to think he was resilient, too. Growing up in his father's house, he'd learned not to complain about his lot, to take life on the chin and get on with whatever was required. Cancer had underlined the lessons in a darker way. Now he had a future to toughen up about. He could not fall in love with Lily. Even if he'd started down the road already, he had to pull back. Now.

He'd start with a shower, breakfast and getting on with the day, making the most of everyone he interacted with, and being friendly but reserved with Lily when she came to the

camp. He would not take the coward's way out
and find another bed to doss down on. He'd try
not to upset Lily, but wouldn't avoid her. They
got on well when he relaxed and stopped overthinking everything.

When Lily joined him in the recreation hall for
the wheelchair races she asked, looking directly
at him, no expectation in her gaze, 'Am I cooking for two tonight?'

He had moved in for the week and not turning
up for dinner would be rude. And disappointing for himself. And going against what he'd
intended. 'If that's all right?' It seemed when it
came to Lily he had no control over his tongue
whatsoever.

Surprise filled her big, bright emerald eyes.
'Good.'

His smile seemed to have become a permanent fixture. No wonder he was in trouble. Lily
did this to him, no matter how strong his determination to remain aloof.

CHAPTER SIX

HE SHOULD HAVE stayed at the camp, Max sighed. Dinner had been great, delicious food and tasty wine, comfortable company. He'd brought coffee into the lounge while Lily had banked up the fire. As he'd sat drinking the coffee he'd tried not to look too long at her, but how could he not?

Sprawled across the couch, reading something on her phone, she looked stunning in her tight jeans and that navy jersey draped softly over her breasts. Tension started crawling through him, tightening places where he didn't need constriction. Memories returned of the warm softness of those breasts filling his palms, the curves of her backside under his hands as he'd held her close and driven into her, those long legs wound around his waist, holding him to her as if she hadn't wanted him to withdraw.

Max leapt to his feet. 'Think I'll have an early night,' he grunted.

Lily was instantly on her feet before him. 'Are you all right?'

'No.' Dragging his fingers through his hair, he drank in the sight in front of him. The vibrant colour of her eyes added to the vibrancy of the waves of thick hair spilling over her shoulders. Hair that shone in the light and had been silk to his touch last time he'd slid his fingers through it.

'It's early.' Her voice was husky, and as sexy as hell.

'I know.' He couldn't find it in him to lie and say he'd had a big day and wanted some sleep. He needed to get away before she drove him crazy. Crazier. He sure wasn't telling her *that*. Not while he had a glimmer of common sense left in his head.

'Max? What's up?'

Like he was about to answer. He'd put some air between them. But his feet were weights, holding him to the floor as he drank in Lily. She was beautiful with her cute nose, lips full, smooth, pink cheeks. A pulse in her throat rose and fell in time to the rapid thumping going on under his ribs.

Placing his hands on the curves of her shoulders, he gently brought her closer and lowered his head to kiss her. Just one small, soft kiss. He had to, couldn't resist any more.

Lily pressed closer, her mouth opening under his.

The citrus scent filled his head. Those lips blanked all thought. His mouth opened on hers, his tongue slid inside to taste her. His arms were around her, his thighs pressed against her, his reaction pressing into her belly. Oh, Lily.

Her tongue met his, danced between them. On his back her fingers were digging in. She was on her toes, stretching upward, pushing into his chest with her breasts.

He kept on kissing her. He couldn't get enough. He'd wanted this from the day he'd seen her on the pavement outside the clinic with their patient. Her body felt right pressed into his, melding with him, becoming one. This was what he wanted, needed. And had sworn not to look for.

When he hadn't been looking, Lily had happened, and look where they were. In each other's arms, free to do as they wished. Except, no, he shouldn't. What if he ended up hurting her? He knew little about strong, loving relationships. Relationships that survived no matter what, even cancer. If he screwed up he'd be heartbroken. Yes, he knew that now. He might survive the hurt, though not hurting her. But pulling his mouth away from her, dropping his arms to his sides, stepping back—that was impossible. Drawing in some air, he submitted to his overwhelming need and continued kissing her. Time became immeasurable.

Then slowly Lily drew her mouth away, gasping for air. 'Max?' she whispered. 'What's going on?' A huge question sat in her eyes. Her arms remained around him, holding tight.

'I want you.'

She was watching him with an intensity that didn't bode well.

Did she see his uncertainty about the future? There wasn't any about wanting her. But his promise to himself was rising again, waving a red flag. Lily would see that, even if she didn't understand. Especially how he'd reacted to their kisses. The loving way he held her, the excitement that would be in his face and at the front of his jeans.

'I want you, too.' Now her arms left him, her body pulled back as she dropped back onto her feet. 'There is a but, isn't there?'

She could read him better than he'd expected. With his fingers, he massaged his scalp. 'Not about taking you to bed and making love. Not at all.'

'Then why are we standing out here?'

'I don't want a repeat of last time.'

Her eyes widened with disbelief. And something more. Surprise? Or understanding? Because she felt the same? What did he tell her? The truth. All of it? Or be selective? Admitting his loving feelings wasn't wise. If she reciprocated in any small way he'd have given hope that he'd then have to shoot down by telling her why he'd never get into a permanent relationship.

Taking Lily's hand, he said, 'Join me on the couch. I've something to tell you.'

'This is serious.'

'Yes, it is.' His heart was thudding, the rhythm rough. If only they hadn't reached this point, had pretended all was okay, he could've continued kissing and sucking up her passion and sexiness and gentleness and… And everything about her.

'Do your kisses usually move in this direction?' A worried smile came his way.

'You'll be the first woman I've talked to about this.' It was too late to pull out. Lily dropped onto the couch and shuffled that cute butt to one end. 'I'm all ears.' No smile of any kind now, but deep concern was coming his way.

The last thing he needed was Lily feeling sorry for him. Sinking down beside her, Max stared at his outstretched feet. 'You asked why I changed specialties. My answer was true, but how that came about is because I loathe being stuck inside buildings and not having a sense of the outside world.' He paused.

Lily briefly rested her palm on his thigh. 'Go on.'

Covering her hand with his, the tension in his gut lightened. He needed her strength, her resilience. He needed Lily. Which was frightening. He had spent most of his life fighting not to need his parents, or anyone else. So why Lily? But why *not*? She was strong, took none of his nonsense, and could be tender towards him.

'Max?'

'Sorry.' He shook his head. 'Three years ago I had cancer.'

Her hand jerked under his.

'Bowel cancer. I had surgery, chemo, radiotherapy and then a new treatment that's still being trialled.'

'That explains the hair.'

'You didn't think I'm going grey because I work my butt off all the time?' It wasn't hard to smile at her.

'I thought you looked like you've been through something awful. I was right, though not about the reason. Max, your news is shocking. How did you cope? Did you stay in Auckland?'

'I went back to Dunedin, mainly because my

family's there, though not all together.' And they had done their best to rally round, but none of them had been used to being so close and talking about serious issues.

'I wanted to get away from everyone I worked with so I didn't have to put up with their sympathy. It didn't take long to realise that'd been a mistake. Most of you would've given me a lot of support in the form of bad jokes and always visiting when I needed to sleep.'

She flicked a grin on and off. 'This happened while I was still in town? Now I think about it, I did hear you'd left the emergency department.'

He nodded. 'You'd just moved to an emergency clinic on the North Shore.'

'Filling in time before going to Singapore.' Shaking her head, Lily asked, 'Where are you now with the cancer? I'm presuming you're all right and waiting for the all-clear.'

If only it was that simple. *It could be if you let it.* 'Yes. And no.' When she fixed that concern on him again, he hurried on. 'I am healthy, fit and have no symptoms. It isn't easy to let go the fear of cancer returning, though. I've got a little way to go for the all-clear, and I hope when that happens I'll move forward with being positive.'

'You already are. Did you not hear yourself? You said when the all-clear happens. Sounds positive to me.'

Her tender smile pierced his heart when he didn't have a heart to give, despite his growing feelings for Lily. He needed her in his life. Standing up, Max paced across the room, returned to sit down closer. 'I hadn't thought of it like that. Not that it changes a thing. I worry that if I do get ill again I could hurt anyone I become close to.'

'Not even if you hurt someone by walking away when she wanted to be with you?'

Was she talking about herself? Or speaking generally? 'Better sooner than later.'

Suddenly she was staring at him hard. Searching for something. What was the question? He might be able to save her from whatever was causing this. 'Lily? What is it?'

She shook her head. 'No, it doesn't matter.'

'Come on. Spill. I've told you something I never share.'

For minutes he thought she was going to ignore him. Then her chest rose, fell and she faced him. 'You indicated you weren't going to have a family. Does that mean you could if you wanted?'

Where was this going? This wasn't something he'd expected to talk about when he'd started down this track, but he may as well tell her. It couldn't hurt. 'My sperm's in the bank. I didn't want to do it but my oncologist talked me into it by saying best to cover the options, and that a time might come when I'd regret not doing so, and if I didn't nothing was wasted. So I gave in and went ahead.'

'You don't think you will have children, do you?'

'I have no intention of it.'

His own kids? His heart squeezed painfully. It would be super-fantastic to be a dad. But what if he left them without a father? 'I don't want to leave my kids without a dad, and that could happen if the cancer returns.'

'Kids lose their parents for all sorts of reasons. Wives lose their husbands, too. You might live till you're ninety and be as grumpy as hell. That's far more likely than you having a relapse.' Her smile had returned, but it wasn't as straight and happy as before. More as though there was still a question lurking in the background.

'Thanks for your support,' he muttered.

'You're welcome.' She stood up. 'That coffee's not doing me any good. I'm making hot chocolate. Want one?'

Was this the end of the discussion? He wasn't sure whether to be pleased or disappointed. 'I'd love one.' The whole telling Lily thing had gone more smoothly than he'd expected. 'Why did you ask that particular question?'

* * *

Lily carefully spooned chocolate granules into mugs while the milk heated in the microwave. Could she tell him? With his fear of the cancer returning, he'd probably be furious if she offered to have his child, say she didn't understand. Which she didn't, quite. But he'd want to be a part of the child's life if she used his sperm. He thought that if he fathered a child it could be left without a dad but she wasn't planning on having a father in the picture anyway. At least she hadn't been until Max had come back into her life.

The romance had been growing on her side, and that had started her thinking they could do this together. Now that romance and his statement of no children reminded her of Leo. They'd supposedly been in love and he hadn't told her he didn't want children.

But Max wasn't Leo. He hadn't held back from telling her anything so far. It was early days, but now she understood he probably never would admit to it if he ever fell for her. He was set on remaining single and not involving children in his life in case the worst happened. For that, she could only admire him and believe in him more than ever. But despite that, the idea of Max as the father of her child was growing stronger every day. As were her feelings for him, and that might make having his child and remaining uninvolved impossible.

Not long ago she'd thought they'd barely be able to tolerate each other and now she was wondering about asking if he'd have a baby with her. If that's what a few heated kisses did then she'd better pull on her wet suit for the duration of his time here. It was hard work getting the tight-fitting suit off at the best of times. A passion-killer for sure.

'I don't like it when you go quiet.' Max half laughed, half growled. He'd shared a lot, and now the doubts over his actions would be setting in.

'Just assimilating everything.' Glancing across to the lounge, she found him watching her far too closely.

'It's a biggie.' He nodded.

'Why you? When you were young and fit? A doctor even. Yes, I get that's irrelevant, but hell.'

'Thank you.' He slumped. 'I thought I was strong, but listen to me whinging like someone stole my ice cream.'

'Come on, Max. You are strong. You took a massive hit, but you're here, getting on with life, if not in the way you might've once envisioned. I haven't been in your shoes, but it seems extreme to not want to try for a happy future that includes your own family. If that's what you want.' It was becoming important that he did for himself, not her.

'You're right.' He turned away.

The microwave stopped and Lily retrieved the milk, poured it into the mugs and stirred vigorously. 'Here you go.' She sat at the table, elbows on top and her chin resting in her hands as she waited for Max to join her. *If* he joined her.

'I saw wives and husbands visiting their terminally ill spouses, kids seeing their parents fading away before their eyes. It was horrific. The brave faces, the downright sad ones, the despair and the hope. I do not want to put anyone I love through that.' He slid onto the opposite chair.

She tentatively sipped the hot drink. 'Who was with you through those months?' Did he have siblings? Parents still alive?

'My sister and her husband were incredibly supportive, my mum stepped up in her own way, making sure I had whatever I needed, which was nice.' He shrugged. 'Dad was a surprise. He dropped in for a few minutes every day, said little or nothing and went away again.'

'A man of few words?'

'Very few, but he did tell me he was proud I'd become a doctor. At first it hurt he wouldn't talk about the cancer but after he said that I realised he'd never known how to say what was in his heart. It was a relief really, though I still wish he'd been a little more open with me as a child.'

Talk about making up years of silence. 'Go, you.' There was nothing to say that wouldn't sound trite.

Max gaped, then laughed. 'Oh, Lily, I don't think I'll ever fully understand you.'

Sounded like a great arrangement to her. It might help to remember she wasn't looking for love again, only a DNA donor. Which didn't explain why daily that idea was twisting into something new, deeper, and filled with love. 'We see lots of tragedies in our everyday lives as doctors, but facing it personally... Well...' she raised one shoulder, let it fall away '... I haven't a clue how I'd react.'

'That's another reason I wanted to change direction in my career. Surgeons spend little time with their patients while they're conscious. Over time GPs see and hear more about what's behind a patient—family, career or interests, illnesses, mind-sets. I also need a window to look out at the sky and trees and traffic, and that allows the light into the dark corners.' His eyes were haunted. 'I like to use the understanding I've gained to help my patients through whatever they have to face.'

She touched his hand. 'You're incredible. You know that? I bet it still isn't easy.' Lily's stomach tightened. Nothing was. Even if she decided she wanted Max as her sperm donor, she didn't have the right to ask him. He deserved better, to have his own needs recognised and accepted, not wrecked to satisfy hers. She didn't want to hurt Max. 'You've had a lot to contend with.'

'Who doesn't at some point in their lives? Anyway, let's drop this. It's too maudlin, and I prefer being cheerful.'

'Then drink your chocolate. It'll put a smile on your face.' While giving her a moment to move past thinking of Max as a likely prospect for a father. His smile was reappearing, bringing a storm of need rushing through her. One night wouldn't be enough. One night would lead to trouble, have her wanting to spend more and more time with Max, and then what? As he'd said, the day would come when he'd call it off—if she didn't first to save her heart like last time. Only this time it'd be harder to do. She was beginning to think Max had always been the man for her, that she'd been in denial even when she'd been with Leo.

Max was smiling. 'I feel like a child when I drink this. My mum used to make it for me and my sister sometimes.'

Lily's heart lurched. He'd had it hard, growing up, which explained some of the sadness in his eyes when he was far away. Again she laid her hand over his. This sitting around talking to Max was becoming their new norm. Yet as much as she wanted to know all there was about him, she wouldn't return the favour. Not yet. Collecting the mugs, she stood and went to rinse them. 'I'm turning in. It's early but I've got a good book on the go.'

Max leaned back in his chair, stretching his legs under the table and tapping the tabletop with his forefinger. 'I'm *that* boring?' he asked through one of those devastating smiles she lusted after.

'Not at all.' But a woman had to do what she could to avoid getting into situations she'd have trouble extricating herself from. Like those kisses. Just thinking about them made her knees weak and her hip press against the bench for support. They'd been moments from heading down the hall to her bed. Max had been hard, pressing against her like he'd never wanted to pull away.

'I thought not.' Max stood up. Came close. Lowered his head so his mouth hovered over hers. 'A goodnight kiss, then?'

Lily swallowed.

'Yes or no?' Max whispered.

'Damn you,' she growled. 'No.'

Liar, shrieked her body. *I want every bit of him.* But she had to resist. Kissing would lead to making love, and then she'd be in big trouble. She was not ready. Forget the need filling her every moment she was with Max. She could still get hurt. 'Sorry,' she whispered, and turned away.

He opened his eyes wide, studied Lily's tense shoulders, straight back and clenched hands at her sides. 'Why, Lily?'

'Because I am not ready for another relationship.' She turned back to him, confusion puckering her face. 'Wrong. I'm not getting into another at all.'

'I was only thinking of tonight.'

Sadness filled her eyes. 'I guessed as much, and while that fits with what I've just said, I can't do it.'

He reached for her hand, unwound her fingers. 'Come and sit down. I don't want to end tonight on this note.'

She stood staring at him for what seemed a lifetime. Who knew what was whirling around in her mind? But finally she nodded, pulled her hand free and headed for the couch to drop down and grab a cushion, which she held close to her chest.

Slowly sinking down on the chair opposite, Max thought how he was going to talk to her about this without giving too much of himself away. He drew a breath. 'I didn't know I'd missed you until that night of the farewell party. Standing in the doorway to Reception, watching you chat to people like you'd known them for ever, it was as though something solid from the past had returned, giving me hope.'

Now she'd be getting ready to kick him out of the house. He hadn't made any sense at all, except to himself. 'We had our differences. Yet those are what I missed. You didn't care what I thought about your opinions, just kept handing them out. It was refreshing, and I didn't understand that's what I'd enjoyed until you turned up that night.'

Shut up. There's explaining and there's talking far too much.

Her fingers were digging hard into that cushion. 'Yes, that was Max. The Max I once knew intimately.' Then she lifted a finger, doubt lingering in her face. 'But he doesn't *sound* like the man I thought I knew.'

'We didn't know each other. Not really.'

Lily tensed. The sound of waves hitting the beach filled the room. Light gusts of wind stirred the trees in the back yard and then she relaxed. 'You used to infuriate me about many things. No doubt I did the same in return.' Her head tipped back against the couch. 'In the intervening years I've wondered where you were, what you were up to.'

'Snap.'

Her breasts rose and she slowly lowered her head to lock eyes with him. 'I had to finish our fling, Max. We were fantastic in bed, no disagreements, all about giving and taking, but I couldn't see how it could lead to anything but trouble. Our relationship wasn't that great, except for those few nights, and I didn't want us ending up arguing in bed.'

He smiled. He couldn't help himself. 'We would've eventually. It was a given. We both had our own ways of getting through life and they weren't compatible. I was selfish.' He was comfortable with Lily in a way he'd never been. He'd told her about the cancer and how it had affected his hopes for the future when he didn't readily tell anyone. Only his sister and one of his closest friends knew how he'd shut down on wanting a wife and kids. And now Lily did. Who was single and building on her career like there were no other plans for *her* future. Had her ex hurt her that badly? She'd be a great mum if the interactions with Josie he'd seen were anything to go by. 'You ever think about having kids? You'd be great at it.'

Lily stiffened, gripping the cushion even harder, pushing back further into the couch, making a chilly gap between them that did not bode well.

'Lily? It was a compliment.' Were there problems for her around having a baby?

'Thank you,' she muttered.

From what he could see, her face was now devoid of emotion. Which told him a lot was going on in her head. 'Talk to me.'

Silence.

He could manage that, too. He waited, forcing the growing tension to back off, ignoring the questions that kept blinking into his mind. There was no point trying to guess what had upset Lily about his statement. He'd only make matters worse.

Her voice was thick, heavy. 'It's so strange you should say that tonight.'

That he'd paid her a compliment or that she'd make a great mother? He waited for more.

Lily rubbed her palms together, laid her hands on her knees, went back to holding the cushion. 'Please hear me out before you comment.'

The seriousness in her voice and face nearly had him telling her she didn't have to say anything if she didn't want to. The moment she told him what was on her mind he knew there'd be no avoiding a truth he might not want to hear, let alone accept. But this was a new relationship for them, one where he didn't poke fun at her and instead listened and helped if possible. 'Go on,' he answered with as much gravity as he'd heard in her voice.

'I do want to be a mother, have a child of my own.' Her breast rose, held there for a long time. As it fell back into place the words gushed from her mouth. 'On my own. I'm not interested in another relationship. I've had two failures. There's only so much rejection and hurt I can take.'

He should be pleased to hear she wasn't interested in a permanent relationship because he'd always know he was safe if they were to continue what they'd started tonight. But he wasn't pleased. Not one bit. Disappointment rattled him, shocking in its intensity. Why, when he wasn't going for permanency? 'Two mistakes doesn't necessarily mean the next time you fall in love it won't work out.'

'I'm not prepared to risk it. Anyway, you're not meant to be commenting, at least until I've finished what I've got to say.' Another pause. 'This might shock you. I am looking to see if I can find a sperm donor I can agree to. It's freaky, but I so want to be a mum. If I can't have a husband or partner who loves me then I'll go it alone. It won't be easy, especially as I'll continue working, but it's been done before and I'll manage.' She drew another breath.

'You probably think I'm being selfish, that all kids deserve, need two parents, and to an extent you're right. But there're plenty of kids out there with one parent and who are growing up surrounded in love and support. That's my promise to any child I'm lucky enough to have.'

Her eyes hadn't left him throughout the whole time she'd been talking. Looking to see if he flinched, or flattened his lips, or got angry? Then she should be surprised because he felt nothing but admiration. 'You're one gutsy lady.' It would be hard, lonely and difficult to juggle work and a baby, but if anyone could raise a child alone and do it well, then here she was.

One well-shaped eyebrow lifted and her gaze lightened. 'Safe answer?'

'Absolutely.' Max itched to brush the stray strands of hair that had fallen over her face. 'Seriously, it's no surprise about you wanting to take on such a huge project.' He put a finger to her lips when she made to speak. 'That's not being derogatory. This will be a lifelong commitment, more than anything you've undertaken before or probably ever will.' Lily wanted a child, and needed a donor for that to happen.

Was this why he'd given in to the oncologist's suggestion of saving his sperm in case he changed his mind about becoming a father? But even if he got over his hang-ups and offered his sperm he'd be worried about leaving his child behind later. If he wasn't prepared to follow through on his feelings for Lily then he sure as hell wasn't offering to be the genetic father of her baby. 'I take it you've done a lot of thinking and research about this?'

'Loads.' Lily relaxed enough to tuck her legs under her backside. 'You continue to astonish me with your belief in what I do. I only hope you're right.'

Tonight had been an evening of opening their hearts to each other. Strange how much more relaxed about everything that made him feel. The edginess he'd carried since his treatment had quietened. Not disappeared, but it was definitely less apparent. Long may that last. 'You won't let your child down, Lily.'

'My biggest problem is fear of letting myself down.'

'Both those men really did a number on you.' His heart ached for her. How could two men have been so cruel to beautiful Lily? Was he biased, by any chance? Of course he was. The thought of anyone hurting her drove him mad.

'They did, but I'm over them and getting on with what's important to me.'

'You think you're over them when you've altered your dreams for the future because of how they treated you?'

'That's enough, Max. I have told you more than I'd once have thought possible. Don't think it gives you the right to start telling me where I'm going wrong.' She said it with a smile, but there was steel running through the words. Steel best not ignored.

'Okay. Think I'll turn in.' He wouldn't get any sleep, but he couldn't sit here with Lily any longer. She pulled him in, made him hungry. He wanted her beyond reason, yet he also wanted to make her happy, not only in the physical way but in every way possible. That just wasn't going to happen so it was best he give up now while he was ahead. *Ha.* Ahead of what? Already his body craved her and his mind taunted him with what could be if he let go the past. Forget being ahead. He was so far behind it was painful.

CHAPTER SEVEN

LILY'S ARMS WERE tense from the vibrations coming from the chainsaw as she sized up another tree that had come down during last weekend's storm. This one was at the back of the camp where no one usually went. It could stay there for another time, but she needed something to concentrate on that didn't have anything to do with Max and what she'd told him last night.

Pulling the goggles over her eyes, she chose the first branch to remove and set to work, focusing on the tree and how it was balanced on strong branches and not wobbling as the saw slid effortlessly through her target. The branch fell to the ground. One down. The second one was as easy. A well-sharpened blade made life a lot easier.

She sighed. If only it was as easy to fix the niggling sense of hope for her and Max finding their way to each other. Fix as in get together romantically or get on with their lives separately, not this hovering in between state. They'd come so close to kissing and making love last night that she still couldn't breathe properly. Her head ached with need, her heavy heart thumped with sadness, and she'd berated herself all night for saying no.

To have said yes would've been wonderful, and brought on another headache, only this one filled with worry that she was already on the slippery slide into love and loss and pain. Max was getting to her, and it was getting harder all the time to maintain her resolve not to fall in love again.

But she wasn't here to think about Max. Attacking the next cut too hard, she slowed, drew a breath and continued more carefully.

A while later she paused to study the pile she'd made. Not a bad morning's work. Killing the motor, she put the saw aside, relishing the sudden quiet. Then her skin tightened. She wasn't alone. Spinning around, she relaxed enough to be friendly. 'Max. Hello.'

'Morning.' He sauntered towards her.

She wasn't fooled. There was a wariness in his gaze, in the way he was tightening and loosening his fingers at his sides. He needn't worry. She wasn't raising the subject of last night's conversations. She'd opened her heart about having a child, and he hadn't laughed or thrown it back at her. When they weren't in sexual overdrive they were getting on so well it was amazing. So much so she'd had to get away while it all sank in, and she figured where she was going with this. Yet he'd found her and that made her happy. Damn it all. She wasn't supposed to happy about that. 'Did you have breakfast here?'

'Yep. Thought I'd stay out of your way for a bit. Obviously not for too long, though.' His smile warmed her throughout. 'How're you today?'

Happy. Confused. Worried. Happy. 'Just fine.' It all came down to Max how good she felt. And confused, and worried, and happy. 'Aren't you refereeing a game this morning?'

He shook his head. 'Everyone's inside for talks until eleven. Logan suggested I come over and see if you needed help moving this. Looks like I'm too late. Want a coffee instead?'

When she nodded, he picked up the saw and walked beside her towards the camp kitchen.

Loud shouts of laughter reached her ears. 'Morning break for everyone. Let's move it.' She picked up her pace and Max matched her. Kind of in sync. As they were becoming about a lot of things. They'd been fully in sync when they'd made love. *Sex, Lily. Not making love.* The love word didn't come into anything to do with Max, then or now. Even if she wanted it to, it couldn't. He'd made it clear he wasn't looking for a woman to share his life with. And she'd done exactly the same in different words, for different reasons. Yet it felt as though neither wanted that any more.

He'd make a wonderful father.

She slowed. Yes, he would. *But he wasn't going to be one.* He'd saved his sperm. *He didn't want to use it.* He might change his mind. *He might not.* He could be her donor. *He'd probably say that was too weird.*

Max slowed for her to catch up. 'Where've you gone?'

Wouldn't he like to know? Probably not. It would be too much. 'Dreaming of a hot scone soaked in melted butter.'

Max laughed. 'I hope you're in luck.'

The plates were still half-full of scones, and the coffee pot in the kitchen for the staff had just been refilled. Sinking onto a chair, Lily stretched her legs and rolled her shoulders. A tightness had built up from holding the chainsaw so long.

'Sore?' Max asked.

She hadn't seen or sensed him coming into her space. *Slipping, Lily.* Though it meant she'd managed to get him out of her mind, however briefly. 'Overworked.'

His smile let him straight back under her

guard. If only she had led him down to her bedroom. She jerked. *Stop it, Lily. This is not the time to be reminiscing about last night*. She'd spent the last hour or more ignoring all the hot, exciting sensations Max had woken in her last night. Hell, any time he came near every one of those sensations filled her.

Was she falling for him? She tensed.

'Relax. I'll get you some food.'

Closing her eyes, she drew a calming breath. Was she? Could she? He never left her mind, turned her on with a glance. She felt at ease with him, wanted more time together. But she was afraid to try again, doubted it'd work out this time any better than the previous two times. If she was starting to get serious about Max she was setting her heart up to be hurt again. Anyway, Max was against getting entangled with anyone or having a family. Surely, deep down, he must want to grab life and run with it? Did he need someone to grab his hand and show him the way? If so, was she ready for that?

'Dr Max, Ollie's had an accident.' Josie was shoving her way through people to get to him. 'Come quick.' She spun around. 'Auntie Lily, you come, too.'

Leaping to her feet, Lily banged her mug down and joined Josie as she raced alongside Max. 'What's happened?'

'We were chasing the soccer ball and he got caught in a hole and went down. I think he's twisted his knee.' Tears streaked down Josie's cheeks. 'He's hurting a lot. He says he's all right. Like I believe him.'

Lily reached for her hand. 'Max will take good care of him.'

'What about you, Auntie Lily? You're the best.'

Max tapped Josie on the arm. 'Thanks, pal.'

'She is,' Josie protested. 'When I knocked myself out on the hay bailer, Lily wouldn't let anyone move me until she'd put something round my neck. Then she got me to hospital real fast.'

Lily hugged her as they raced over the lawn towards a group of teenagers. 'Max is very good, too. *And* he's the camp doctor, not me. I promise Ollie's in good hands.' So was she while she sorted herself out. If she committed to Max, fell in love with him, it would be for ever. If he returned that love, she'd be safe. It was a big if, though. He was so doubtful about his future. And to be fair, she wasn't one hundred percent certain of her own, was still wary of handing over her heart only have it squashed again.

'Okay, clear a space, guys,' Max said as he pushed through the onlookers and knelt down.

'Ollie, I hear you put your foot in a hole while running after the ball.'

Ollie groaned. 'It was a rabbit burrow. I heard a pop as I fell. My knee looks odd.'

'It hurts?'

'Yeah, some. My foot's swelling. The shoe's too tight.'

Max said, 'I'll remove it.' As he was doing that, he was appraising the knee in front of him. 'You've sprained your knee. What I'm not sure about is if there's a torn ligament or not. That popping sound suggests there might be.'

It was good how Max was being up front with him, not treating him like a child, which was a tendency with some people when with the physically disabled.

'Josie? You up for bringing me water and food when I need it? And fetching my phone or a jacket?' Ollie teased.

Josie bit her lip, looking worried. Then she giggled. 'Absolutely not. Then you'd be wanting me to wipe your…' She broke off, looking embarrassed when she glanced at Max.

'Trust me, there's nothing wrong with his arms.' Max grinned. 'Okay, Ollie, first we need to get you inside and raid the freezer for ice to pack around your knee. Then I'll phone for an MRI appointment, which might be a couple of days away. In the meantime you should try walking normally, though not too often straight up.'

'So nothing too bad going on?'

'It'll be painful for a while, but more a nuisance than anything.' Max stood up. 'As long as common sense prevails and you don't decide to go for a run.'

'When I need your advice I'll have to crawl to you.'

Lily smiled. The young man had strength and a sense of humour. Josie had done all right first time round. Glancing at her niece, her smile increased. Yes, Josie was smitten. Her eyes were full of love and her face lit up with a full-on smile. She might be lucky and, like her parents, have found her life partner at an early age. No one could predict how these things worked out, especially not her aunt.

Lily's gaze tracked to Max who, with the help of other boys, was getting Ollie up onto his good foot. Max had been straightforward about the injury, hadn't downplayed it, or built it up to reinforce the need to be careful. Ollie could make his own decisions, to a point.

There was a squeezing in her chest. Max was coming up trumps from every angle, making it impossible to deny the burgeoning hope in her heart that she could try for a relationship again. Not only have a baby, but a man in her life.

Ducking her head, she wiped her cheek. Could she be so lucky? Max and their baby? Her chest sank as her stomach tightened in on itself.

Could her dreams come true? Why not? *Let go, and see what happens.* Her heart softened as her gaze followed him up the lawn with the boys. Okay, yes, she was falling for him. Wait. Wasn't this a similar feeling to that she'd known when she and Leo had been starting out? It was nothing like it. That time there hadn't been a sense of coming home, of having found exactly what she wanted, required, loved.

Turning to stare out over the grassed field to the quiet sea, Lily contemplated her feelings for Max. Letting *him* down wasn't an option. The first flush of love in both her previous relationships had come with an easy acceptance of everything about the men, no deep thought had gone into it. It had felt right so she'd gone along with the excitement and love. With Max there was history, not all good, but it showed him to be rock solid when it came to giving his all to any person or project he undertook. That gave her confidence he wouldn't change his mind and want out of a relationship, if he ever got over his fears enough to let love reign his heart.

'Auntie Lily, what are you doing? We're going inside.'

'Ollie doesn't need me. Max knows what he's

doing so I'm going for a walk.' Wrapping her arms around Josie's thin frame, she kissed the top of her head. 'Go spend time with Ollie. He's being brave but he needs you.'

'You like him?'

'Of course I do.'

'Cool. See you later.' Josie was gone, bounding inside as though afraid of missing a minute with Ollie.

Lily walked to the beach and headed in the direction of the house. The fresh, cool air was good on her face, the increasing silence just what her frazzled mind needed.

Max.

He'd sneaked into her mind, body, everywhere, when she had least expected him. She had to decide whether to get over him for ever or take a chance. She had no idea if he'd join her in that risk, but if she did lay her heart on the line, it would be with everything she had. And it felt as if her heart had already made up its mind.

'There you go,' Max said as he wound the ice bag around his young patient's knee. 'Now, what I said about this not being a major injury is true—to a point. You can wreck it further if you get too exuberant physically. A little often is the way to go.'

'I hear you, Doc.'

'I'll make sure he behaves,' Josie added, sitting as close to Ollie as possible without being on top of him. 'Auntie Lily's gone for a walk along the beach. That way...' She pointed a thumb in the direction of the beach house. 'She wasn't looking happy. I think you should see what's wrong,' she said with a cheeky smile.

Little minx. 'I've got a physio session with some of your pals shortly, so I'll be hanging around here.' What was wrong with Lily? She'd seemed to have got over last night's black moment. Had he said something else to upset her? Nothing came to mind. As far as he knew, they were getting along just fine. More than fine if their intense conversations last night were anything to go by, if the way he couldn't stop thinking about her and them being together a lot more was an indicator. 'I'll leave you two to fill in the rest of the day and see what's happening in the hall.'

First, he'd get some fresh air. Glancing at his watch, he saw he had fifteen minutes to spare so headed down to the beach and began striding out in the opposite direction from the beach house.

Lily. She was so sexy she blew his mind away. He got lost in her just being in the same room. His heart had taken hours to calm after she'd said no to a kiss. Then her revelation about wanting to have a child on her own had been a gut-buster. It underlined her determination not to get involved with another man, yet there was passion oozing out of her when they were together. It wasn't any of his business she was thinking about getting pregnant. He couldn't do that for her.

Pain ripped out of his mouth, roared through the air.

No, he couldn't. Yet he had to. Or take a chance, ask her to take a chance.

An image of them lying naked on his bed three years ago, their bodies intertwined after making love, slammed him. What was it about Lily that these images came as quickly as a blink? With a reaction in his groin that needing satisfying. He couldn't get enough of her body, her sexiness, the gentle touches she gave him, the kisses filled with longing and more. Sharing and caring. And more. Something he refused to identify because then he'd have to face up to facts and he just wasn't ready for that.

Was he ready to give up? Not kiss Lily again? Not to hold her in his arms and soak up the heat she gave him; heat that overtook the cold that had sat in his heart from the day he'd decided never to look for love? Not to sit together over a coffee or a wine while talking about anything and everything? Sharing their hearts? Their dreams?

Max kicked a convenient pebble down to the water. No, damn it, he didn't want to give that up any more. Especially as she'd shared something so personal and dear as wanting to have a baby. He kicked another, larger pebble and grimaced at the sharp pain in his toes.

Lily, Lily, Lily. You always did my head in. Only this time it's for different reasons. You're softer, funnier, more accepting, more compelling. I like you. I love...

Max swore. Wrong. Wrong. Another stone splashed into the sea. They were getting along just fine as they were. *Leave it at that. Don't bring in the heavy emotions. Don't bring in the baby idea.* That would only lead to trouble.

On Thursday, Max's last night before he headed back to the city, Lily placed plates in the oven to warm for dinner, though so far he was a no-show. Not even a text to say he was running late as he had last night. Something must've happened to one of the children. They were all getting a little too exuberant as the week passed.

After pouring a small glass of wine, she added wood to the fire, and sank onto the couch with her legs tucked under her. Tomorrow was Friday. Come Monday she'd be ensconced in the Remuera Medical Hub, getting on with her career where Max would be part of the scene. How much importance had he put on what she'd said about having a baby? He'd better not think she'd been hinting for his involvement.

A shudder ran the length of her spine. She wanted a baby so much, but over the past days the need had begun taking second place to wanting to be with Max. It was still hard to believe she'd pulled away from kissing him. Especially when she'd wanted to so badly. Longed for his kisses, dreamed of them. To have given in would have been to hand herself over to him and trust he wouldn't hurt her when he'd said he wasn't getting into a relationship.

She had to concentrate on having a child, not on losing her heart to a man. She'd love her baby completely and utterly. No doubts whatsoever. Just because there wouldn't be a real, live father on the scene it didn't mean her child would go without love from the males in her family. Try keeping her brothers out of the picture. Impossible. They'd be backed up by their own children too. She sighed. She'd gone through this time after time and always came up with the same certainty. It was fine to have a child as a solo parent. She would be a good mother.

But there was Max. She felt connected to him in a genuine caring and sharing way. There was love there too, though she wasn't admitting how involved her heart was. It was taking over from the ticking biological clock urging her to become a mother. As if she'd come full circle and wanted the man, the romance and then a child would follow from shared love.

Damn, this was difficult. What to do? Max had become important to her future, her plans, herself. She wanted to be the same for him. He had hurdles to overcome if there was ever going to be a happy outcome for him. She wanted that to be with her.

Follow your heart. It was already involved with Max so had little to lose. Lily drained her glass. So much for a small drink. She needed more. Where was he anyway? Dinner would be ruined soon. Opening the oven, she lifted out the plates and a dish of thick creamy sauce and set them on a board. She wasn't waiting any longer.

'That smells delicious.'

She spun around. 'I didn't hear you come in.' How long had he been here? Thud, thud inside her chest. How could she have missed him? Whenever she was near Max her pulse had a way of speeding up. Not tonight apparently. Though it was making up for lost time now.

'I drove up about twenty minutes ago and got waylaid by George wanting to talk about Archie and how he's really in the doldrums about Enid. Thinks it's his fault she's not coming right as he was over here instead of at home.'

'Nothing unusual in that. But I can understand his point. Enid's everything to him, and he'll be lost if she doesn't make it home again.' It was good George had talked to Max. Especially when those men were so stubborn about talking about anything personal.

'I gathered that.' Max opened the fridge to retrieve the wine bottle they hadn't finished on Monday night. 'Top up?'

'A small one.' Now Max was here she'd take it quietly. Spilling her mind was not happening. Since it was the last night he'd be sharing the house she wanted to make the most of it. Who could have known that they would share such intimacy? Not only the physical kind, not the kisses that'd turn her into a riot of heat and need and hope. But talking about hopes and dreams and what had gone wrong in their pasts. She should follow her heart. Get to know everything about him. And if it didn't work out? At least she'd have tried. If it didn't work out, then it didn't. The hurt would be great either way.

Just don't rush Max.

'What's for dinner?' Max asked, then shook his head, looking surprised.

'What?'

'I sound as though this is normal, coming in and asking what we're going to eat.' His lips pressed together as though he needed to stop any more words spilling out. The surprise was being replaced by bewilderment. The wine splashed down the side of the glass he was filling.

By the look on his face, he'd made a blunder and was appalled to have voiced it. That hurt. But this was never going to be easy. Reaching for the glass he handed her, she took a deep sip. Max hadn't meant it to sound like that; it had been a casual reference to sharing the house this week. 'Spaghetti bolognese. Hope you don't mind pasta.'

'When it smells as good as what I'm getting whiffs of, I'll eat anything.' Relief was replacing all the other emotions in his face.

And pouring through her veins. They were getting along far better than she'd ever imagined, and it was good. Better than good. Regardless of the future, colleagues, friends— lovers?—regardless of her indecisions, right now it felt great to be spending an evening with Max, enjoying a wine and meal together. That's what she'd run with and to hell with all those other ideas about love. They could take a hike and leave her to enjoy the night.

* * *

Max leaned a hip against the bench to watch Lily talking with Josie on the phone. There was such love in her face as she spoke to her niece. Her child was going to be very lucky to have Lily as her mother. He couldn't explain why he thought the baby would be a girl. 'She' just kept coming up whenever he thought about the staggering idea Lily had shared.

He was still absorbing the facts. The more he thought about it the more he believed it was a great idea. Another idea had begun lurking at the back of his skull. But he refused to put it into words, even to himself. Then it would be real, and scary.

She held him in her hand, even if she didn't know it. He wanted to cherish her, show her not all men were like those two who'd broken her heart. Unless… No. Don't even think about it. But… Don't. He could always change his mind about becoming a father. About being a husband to the most wonderful woman he'd known.

Lily wants to do it alone because she no longer trusts her heart to any man.

Would he be prepared to help her achieve her dream? What about the ramifications? It wasn't in him to stand back and take no part in his child's life. Lily would do a wonderful job, but it wasn't happening. Wasn't his future planned to be without a child? Without a wife? To become a respected GP and a part of the community—on his own? He had friends to spend time with, could avoid worrying about hurting those nearest and dearest.

That was it, then. No sperm donation. No getting further involved with Lily. His gut ached. Just like that, he could walk away.

He swore. So much for not voicing the idea.

Lily's head shot up and surprised eyes lit on him.

He must have sworn aloud. Gulping the wine, he muttered, 'Sorry. I didn't mean anything by it.' It showed how much she got to him. Come on. If the idea of donating his sperm was alive and bashing around in his skull then she'd not only got to him, Lily had stormed him body and soul and he was in deep trouble.

His gut churned. It was one hell of a pickle. One not so easy to walk away from as others he'd faced. Except the cancer. That had been a game-changer. Now Lily had him in a vice and, yes, this was about the future, the only difference being he held the cards, could choose the outcome. He could squash these heart-warming emotions sucking the pain and loneliness out of him, or he could let go and make the most of Lily and all she had to offer. If she was at all interested in him. His pulse slowed. Was she?

On Tuesday night she'd pulled back from kissing him, yet she'd wanted to as badly as he'd wanted to kiss her. Did she or didn't she want another fling with him? Or was something deeper and more meaningful on her mind? Damn all these questions. They spoiled the moment, were wrecking his last evening with Lily.

Even while she was talking to Josie he was happy to be in her company. It showed how lonely he must have been before this week. And, no, he wasn't getting close to Lily just because he needed someone to spend time with. If that was all, he had mates to talk to. Admit it. Again. Lily was special, and it was getting harder by the day to pretend he wanted to walk away.

They'd got close fast. Heat regularly zapped between them. So did laughter and enjoyment of the everyday things. He could feel a new life opening up before him, a wonderful, happy, exciting one. It made him want to make love and give her pleasure, to share her bed, and hold her afterwards as she fell asleep, to wake by her side in the morning. There was more substance to that than just having a great time and saying thanks and goodbye.

So he didn't just want a fling, then. He could no longer imagine walking away from Lily. She held him in her hand, even if she didn't know it. He wanted to cherish her, show her not all men were like those two who'd broken her heart.

'I think Josie's in love.' Lily tossed her phone on the couch and unwound that long slim body to stand up.

'Definitely. So's Ollie. Has he talked to you yet about their...' he flicked his fingers in the air '..."friendship"?'

'Only to say he hoped I was okay with him spending time with Josie.' Her lips tipped up into a smile. 'I didn't come down like the ogre aunt. Told him it was fine with me.'

'But watch out for her father as his chainsaw is larger than yours.'

'Something like that.' She laughed.

He loved it when she laughed. A deep-bellied sound that slammed into his gut and sent his pulse rate skyward. As did many things about Lily. Things that had him crossing the room to take her face in his hands and lean in for a kiss. A kiss for everything she gave him, for taking away some of his hurt.

A kiss that soon deepened, heated, and became so much more.

A kiss that led to another and another.

A kiss that Lily finally pulled back from, a wobbly smile on her swollen lips. 'Max,' she whispered, laying her hand on his cheek.

Okay, he got it. They had to stop. Frustrating, yet not. She was putting her own needs out there, and strange but he didn't mind. Oh, sure, his body was screaming out for hers, but it was wonderful sharing those kisses without follow-through. As though it was a part of getting to know her better, and understanding her needs. He wound his arms around her and held her close, listening to her even breathing. He wanted to hold her tighter than ever before, to pull her into himself, be one with her, to become a part of her life, make it their life.

A chill covered his hot skin, cooling him fast. *Wrong, Max. You can't do this. What if you get sick again? You'll hurt Lily. And leave that child she wants so badly without a father.*

It wasn't going to have a father if Lily did it her way. But if he were the DNA donor it would, which meant he'd be setting them all up for heartbreak. He couldn't be the means to making Lily achieve her dream. He longed to give his heart and soul to any child of his that came into the world. *And* to the mother of that child. There was only one woman he wanted for that role. He wanted to be the man Lily chose to father her child.

'I have to pinch myself to believe we're together again, and that it's so good,' Lily said quietly.

The chill became colder. He knew what she

meant. He'd gone too far. Already he was in deep water and needed to get out fast. What he longed for and what he accepted as possible were at opposite ends of the spectrum. He could not hurt Lily. It might already be too late for himself. 'I shouldn't have kissed you, Lily.'

Leaning back in his arms, she stared up at him. 'Maybe, but I'm glad you did.'

'We can't carry on further.'

She tensed, stepped out of his arms. 'Did I say we would?'

They had to stop. Impossible. Which said he was already screwed. 'I don't know what you think. Hell, I don't know what *I* think any more.' If he leaned forward he could touch her soft skin, but he refrained, understanding the need for the barrier, if not happy with it. He was supposed to be glad she'd stepped away. He wasn't. Damn, his head was all over the place. 'If I'm honest, I'm not sure where we're headed.'

Silence fell between them.

Then she rocked his boat. 'I know I'm not ready to stop spending time with you. I'd like to get to closer to you. I stopped kissing you because I was about to drag you down to my bedroom and I suddenly got cold feet. But they're warming up fast.' Lily had always spoken her mind. Too bluntly sometimes, but he couldn't fault her.

He shouldn't be surprised, yet he was. Probably because he didn't want to believe she might've learned to like him more than they'd once have imagined. 'I'm not so certain about that. I still have things to consider, like my future.' Starting tonight. If this was how Lily felt—not factoring in his own needs—then it was definitely time to quit whatever they had going on. He wanted her. If only he had a crystal ball and knew he wouldn't get sick again. But no one knew that.

'You think?'

Here we go. This was more like the woman he'd once known. 'I told you I'm not getting into a full-time relationship. What if this turns into something deeper? I don't want to hurt you, so I'm calling it quits as of now. I'm sorry I kissed you.' Pain gripped him. His heart was pounding so hard his ribs felt like they were breaking. If only he could take back those words and reach over and haul Lily into his arms, never to let her go. From the moment he'd uttered them he'd known he did not want to finish anything with her. He wanted a future together, no matter what happened. He flung his arms wide, palms up and shrugged. 'I am so, so sorry, Lily.' If he didn't get out of there right now he might never find the strength to go.

CHAPTER EIGHT

MONDAY MORNING AND the sun was shining. No sign of the clouds that had delivered rain throughout the night. The road and paths sparkled, as though they'd had a thorough wash with bubble-bath liquid.

Lily parked at the rear of the medical hub and pushed open the door before she got too comfortable in her maudlin bubble. The three days since she and Max had discussed—disagreed about—how far they were going with getting to know each other had been long and tedious. Chainsawing more trees into firewood hadn't lightened her mood. Neither had Ollie and Josie when they'd stayed over with her in the house, separate bedrooms, funny and sweet as they were.

Those kisses had whacked her around the ears, made her realise she'd fallen for Max and was ready to take a chance with her heart. They'd scared her senseless so she'd stopped in the middle of a soul-warming kiss and said no more. By the time she'd regained her senses and was ready to apologise, Max had changed his mind about caring—for ever. What a mess she'd made of it all. And now she had to start over. She wasn't letting him get away without a fight.

Max had a way about him that spoke of honesty and kindness and love. She knew he didn't want to hurt her. She also understood the two men who had broken her heart had never held her heart as carefully as Max would if he loved her. And on that she was prepared to take the risk of loving him.

Grabbing her bag off the back seat, Lily locked the car and headed inside. Was Max already here? She needed to get her A-game face in place. Letting him see how devastated she was over what he'd believed were the final words on the subject wasn't an option.

Deep, toe-curling laughter came from the staff meeting room. She had her answer. Her tongue cleaved to the roof of her mouth. Pulling back her shoulders wasn't improving her mood. Max was irresistible. Driving back into the city late last night, she'd headed towards his place to have it out with him, only to turn around at the corner of his street and head home, where she'd realised she'd been scared and that she should have carried on to his house. Well, she'd try again. There was no point arguing. He'd made his mind up. He hadn't changed as much as she'd first thought. That stubbornness had been there in the determined way he'd turned from her and headed for the door and the bedroom next to hers. He believed he would hurt her.

Newsflash, Max, you're already doing that. And I'm not giving up on you.

Yes, she'd gone and fallen for the one man she'd never have believed possible. If he thought he was walking away without a fight, then she had news for him. She'd show him he could live a happy life free of worrying about the pain he might cause her and any children they might have. Of course she'd have a fight on her hands. This was Max. He was worth fighting for, and she was damned if she wasn't going to give it everything she had. It would take time, but she had plenty of that.

Dropping her bag on her new desk, she paused to look around. The walls were bare now that Sarah had removed her diplomas and photos of family, but that wouldn't last. There was a box in the boot of Lily's car filled with her versions of the same things. Warmth finally filled her. She'd made it. Today the next phase of her career was beginning, with Max in the same space. One step towards a joint future achieved without trying. She'd give it a tick for positivity.

In the staffroom she poured a coffee and looked around to say hello to those who'd already arrived. Her gaze immediately landed on Max, looking good in light grey dress trousers and a white shirt. 'You're looking posh.' She grinned, aiming for positivity from the start.

He smiled as he came across. 'Ready to get stuck in?'

'Absolutely.'

'You stay on at the beach house over the weekend?'

'I did. Josie and Ollie stayed Friday night and my brother picked them up on Saturday. He gave Ollie a thorough once-over.'

'How'd that go?' Max sipped coffee and her stomach tightened as she watched those lips she knew so well.

Lips. Kisses. Trails over her feverish skin. Ragged sigh. Slowly, remember, or Max would be bolting for his office and only coming out when he knew she'd left for the day. 'Ollie won the first round just by being himself and not trying too hard to impress.'

'Go, him,' said Max.

'What did you do over the weekend?'

'My sister and her husband were in town for a rock concert so I caught up with them yesterday before they flew back to Dunedin. It was good to see Karen. It's been nearly a year since the last time.' His face had softened and there was a rare relaxation about him. 'She's pregnant for the second time, and absolutely glowing.'

'You miss her?'

He nodded. 'I do. We've always got on, despite the rift between our parents, but it wasn't until I spent time having treatment down there that we became close. She was there for me every single day.' He blinked rapidly. 'I can never repay her for that.'

'You shouldn't have to. You'd do the same for her. For anyone you care about.'

'True, but I'm the older brother. I'm there for her, not the other way round.'

'Excuse me, you're talking to me, the woman with two older, bossy brothers who know how to deal with just about everything, and I'd be there for them any time they needed me, whether they liked it or not.' Her voice rose on the final words, and her throat tightened. Sounded as though she was no different from Max's sister. That had to be a positive for her.

Max locked his steady eyes on her probably less steady ones. 'Easy. I hear you.' Then he smiled again. 'Maybe I shouldn't introduce you and Karen. There'll be no hope for me even if I only wanted an extra piece of cake.'

The tension that had been building backed off. 'Sounds fine to me.' Looking around, she gasped. The room had filled up. 'I'm getting a refill and taking a seat.' First meeting, first day.

'Lily,' Max called quietly. 'Karen will be in town again next month for a work conference. I'll introduce you to her.'

He what? She'd thought they weren't spending time together away from here. Lily coughed, banged her mug on the counter harder than intended, nodding slowly. 'Done.' Maybe she wasn't the only one wanting to make a go of their relationship. Or was he making up for his abrupt departure from the house on Friday morning? Been doing some soul-searching? About them, him, or what he'd said? He'd been heading out the front door with his bag when she'd gone out to make a coffee at six, unable to sleep and needing caffeine to get her out of the fog her head had been in after a sleepless night.

'See you Monday.'

He'd closed the door behind that delectable derriere, leaving her heart mashing and her head spinning. It had taken a whole plunger of coffee to get her anywhere near capable of thinking about the day ahead. Then it had taken some more and toast before she'd allowed herself to pick up the chainsaw and head across to George's yard and the tree trunks he'd towed there from along the beach over the past couple of days. Hours of heavy work had finally worn her out enough to fall into her chair and eat a proper meal.

She'd sat up with the kids until finally she'd been unable to keep her eyes open and had hit her bed to sleep until dawn, when shrieking gulls had woken her to a blinding headache. She'd woken with Max in her head, denying they had a future, and her telling him he was wrong. She'd also recalled Josie and Ollie on the couch, sitting close together, holding hands, and guilt had struck for not making sure they behaved.

When Josie had sauntered out of her room as far as her crutches would allow and sat at the kitchen bench with a grin on her face, Lily had felt she'd let the aunt side of things down, until Josie had laughed and said, 'Relax, Lily. Nothing happened. Apart from my first kiss.' Her cheeks had turned crimson, and her mouth had crinkled up into a soppy smile. 'It was nice. He's cute.'

Lily had put her hands over her ears and laughed. 'Stop. I don't want to know.' Thank goodness nothing too intimate had gone down. Josie might have fibbed, but she was absolutely hopeless at hiding lies, especially from Lily.

And now this morning Max was friendly and back to their new normal.

She'd run with that. Sitting on the closest vacant chair, she joined in the chatter until Devlin got the meeting underway and she began to learn how this medical centre went about its daily business. Max was a part of this, and for now that was enough. Then she took another look. Under the overhead light, shadows below his eyes had become apparent. Lack of sleep, too?

'How long have you had this sore throat?' Lily asked fifteen-year-old Courtenay Griffith.

'All weekend, and some days before that,' muttered the girl dressed in the uniform from the local high school.

'Are you sure?' Lily asked as she put the thermometer in Courtenay's ear. 'Your throat's raw. What about coughing?'

'No, but my neck hurts, gets stiff sometimes.'

'Your temperature's raised.' Lily clicked the end piece off the thermometer into the hazard bin. 'I'm going to check your neck and throat.' Swelling around Courtenay's neck backed up her diagnosis, along with the high temperature.

'What's wrong with me?'

'I'd say you've got glandular fever.'

'Isn't that called the kissing disease?'

'That is the fastest way to transmit it, yes.' Lily smiled as she locked eyes on her patient. 'Have you been kissing anyone?'

'My boyfriend. But that was last weekend. I was too tired to see him this weekend.'

'Has he got a sore throat?'

'He did, then he got better so it can't be what you're saying.'

Lily sat at her desk and began typing notes into the computer. 'Yes, it can. You probably need to tell him so he can see his doctor.' Filling in a lab form on screen, she pressed 'print', signed the page and handed it to Courtenay. 'I want you to have a blood test to confirm this is glandular fever. In the meantime, no more kissing. You'll need to stay home from school for a couple of weeks. Keep indoors, keep warm and get lots of sleep. Drink plenty of water. I'll give you a prescription for antibiotics and pain relief.'

Loud voices came through the door.

Courtenay jerked her head around. 'That sounds like Mum. What's wrong?'

Lily rushed to open the door, and cries filled the room.

'Someone look at Tommy. He's going blue. Hurry,' a woman holding a small child screamed.

Lily rushed to her side, took the lifeless boy from her arms. 'Follow me.' She headed back into her room, the woman right on her heels. 'Tell me what happened,' she demanded as she sat the lad on the bed. His chest moved slowly, his lips were blue. How long had he been unconscious? Tipping his head back to open his throat, she reached for his wrist. Pulse too slow.

'I don't know,' the boy's mother wailed.

'Mum, what's wrong with Tommy?' Courtenay cried.

'Colleen, take a deep breath and tell us what Tommy was doing when this happened.' Max had arrived.

Lily sighed with relief. 'His pulse is faint, he's barely breathing.'

'Onto it.'

'Playing with his toys.'

'What sort of toys?' Lily asked as she placed Tommy on his back and pulled his top up to his chin to place the stethoscope over his lungs.

Max was feeling the boy's throat, looking in his mouth. They weren't about to discuss who did what, they got on with what had to be done.

It was Courtenay who answered. 'He has small blocks he likes to stick in his mouth.'

'How small?' she demanded, reaching to sit Tommy upright.

Max had it under control with his hands under Tommy's arms and holding him steady. He nodded at Lily. 'Heimlich manoeuvre.'

Nodding, she slapped the small back. And again. And once more. Tommy shuddered and a feeble cough spewed over his lips.

'Again,' Max said.

Another, harder slap.

The boy's cough was stronger.

'Come on,' Lily muttered. Her hand was ready for the next blow.

A small square of plastic shot out of Tommy's mouth. Followed by more coughing and lots of slobber. Then he began crying.

Phew. Lily let out the breath she'd been holding. 'There we go.'

Max was examining the boy's mouth, cleaning away the mess inside. 'You're one lucky little guy, Tommy.'

Lily's heart was racing with relief, and she lifted the boy up and handed him to his crying mother. 'Here you are.'

Courtenay was crying, then Tommy joined in and Lily stepped back for a moment, Max standing beside her. 'That was touch and go,' he muttered.

She nodded, and watched the love pouring from the family. 'Mrs Griffith.' She waited until she had the woman's attention. 'I'm Lily Scott, the GP who's replaced Sarah. Now, you mightn't want to hear this, but those toy blocks are dangerous. You have to get rid of them.'

The woman's face was white as she nodded. 'I know. I'll do it when we get home.'

'No, Mum, I'm getting them out of the car and throwing them in the bin before we leave here.' Courtenay wrapped an arm around her mother's shoulders.

'I'm going to examine Tommy's throat, then I'm going to have him admitted to hospital overnight. There's a strong possibility swelling will occur, which can affect his breathing.'

Max added his endorsement. 'Go there immediately. Courtenay, you're right about getting rid of the blocks, but your brother needs to get to hospital first. I know you won't let him near those toys anyway.'

Lily felt a warm glow engulf her. Max was with her, all the way. Medically anyway. Now she had to make it work personally.

Suddenly her room was empty of everyone but Max. 'Thank you for being here. It's not that I wouldn't have coped, but it's always good to have back-up.' Especially when it was this man.

'You're welcome.' He dropped the softest of kisses on her forehead. 'See you soon.' And he disappeared.

After a few minutes, gathering her breath and steadying her nerves, Lily headed out to get her next patient. 'Michelle? Hello, you're looking a lot better than a week ago.'

Michelle smiled shyly as she hopped along beside Lily on her crutches. 'I'm glad you talked me into going there. It was wonderful helping all those kids. They're so positive despite their physical problems, and taught me a thing or two.'

'That was the idea,' Lily admitted as she closed her door behind Michelle and headed to her desk.

'You set me up?' Michelle laughed. 'I like you, Doc. That was clever. Watching those teens getting on with having fun and being as good as they could made me think about my strengths, and realise one of them is about never giving up. I don't understand why I got down this time, but I'm over it and working hard at getting back on my feet.'

'I'm glad to hear it.' Lily brought up Michelle's records on the screen. 'So what can I do for you today?'

Shyness shone back at her. 'Um, I'd like to go on the Pill.'

To put the woman at ease, Lily asked her questions even though the file had the answers. 'Have you been on it before?'

'Yes, about three years ago. I had no problems so I'd like the same one if possible.'

Lily looked at the file. 'It's a good one and I don't think any of the newer brands would serve you any better so that's a yes if your blood pressure's normal.'

'It might've gone up a bit last week.' Michelle glanced up at her, her cheeks burning. 'Logan and I… We get along like a house on fire. He's wonderful.'

It really had been a week of romance. Her

niece and friend were closer than before. Michelle had found a man she obviously fancied like crazy. And she… Well, she'd started falling in love with Max. It didn't add up when they never used to get on very well apart from the fling days. Self-protection? Had she always held herself back from totally giving herself over to men? If so, there was no apparent reason. Her family was loving and close, never let each down. It was more likely she'd hadn't handed her heart over completely before.

'I take it you're going to keep seeing each other, hence the prescription.' It mightn't be how all doctors talked to their patients, but Michelle seemed open to chatting, might even need someone to talk to.

Lily filled in the prescription form on screen. 'Anything else while you're here?'

'No, I'm good. Max is giving me physio this morning.' She stood up, reached for her crutches. 'Thanks for everything, including the camp. I've talked to Logan about helping out another time. I enjoyed it so much.'

'I'm glad. Thank *you*.'

'How's your morning been?' Max asked Lily as he strode into the tearoom well after midday. He'd barely managed one piece of toast for breakfast so to appease his stomach, which no longer ached, he'd dashed down to the bakery to buy a salmon and cream cheese bagel. Sighting Lily at the table, looking completely at ease, lightened his heavy heart. Did her hands just tighten around her mug? He looked again. Saw her fingers loosen. So he did get to her as easily as she got to him.

'It's been great. I've met some lovely people. Michelle saw me before she came to you for physio. She enjoyed her time at the camp and has asked to do more.'

'She was a hit with all the kids. Not to mention Logan. Apparently they've got a thing going for each other.'

'Quite a week, wasn't it? These camps really do help people get over their disabilities.'

'I agree,' Devlin added from the corner, where he was reading a medical journal. 'Max has been singing the camp's praises all morning.'

'I had an amazing time. My medical skills weren't used much, but showing those teens ways to make moving easier, and giving them exercises to do, well, it was just as good as prescribing treatment for any other malady.' He picked up his bagel. 'I want to put my name down for more, too.' The salmon flavour exploded across his tongue. Food, delicious food. Damn, he was hungry. For Lily. Swallow. Cough. Damn.

'Done,' said Lily and Devlin at the same time. *What's done?*

'Devlin's in charge of volunteers.' Lily added, 'In case you weren't aware.'

'I was.' To hell with being hungry. Right now another stronger appetite was winding him up. Need for Lily clawed through him. She looked beautiful sitting there, being herself, not expecting anything from anyone. Heat exploded below his belt. She was gorgeous, and hot, and sweet, and every damned thing he wanted in a woman. *His* woman. His fears for the future annoyed him but were no longer beating him up. It might be unfair to ask Lily to join that ride with him, but hope was rocketing. Lily wanted to have a baby regardless of whether he was in her life or not. *Why not mine?*

He choked. Swallowed. Coughed, swallowed again, and finally downed the food his stomach had been waiting for.

'You all right?' the woman doing his head in asked with concern in her face.

Absolutely wonderful, thanks. 'I'm fine. Lunch went down the wrong way.' He yawned and rubbed his stomach.

Lily was staring at him really hard as though she saw exactly what was going on in his skull. She probably did. The damned woman could read people with her eyes shut. No, she did not know he wanted her to have his baby. She. Did. Not. But he could tell her.

Another choke. This time harder, and painful.

Hands banged him between the shoulder blades, strong fingers dug in. 'Easy. What's going on?'

'Nothing.' Said like a teenager denying the truth. Max tossed the rest of the bagel on top of the bag it had come in. So much for being ravenous. Getting food where it was needed wasn't working. Another need was growing exponentially the longer Lily's hands were on his back. His skin was tightening, heating, and his groin was thickening. As for the rate his blood was pumping around his body, it would burst out of his skin any moment. He held his breath. And waited. Leaping up to get away from that sincere touch would be best, but would probably earn him so many demerit points he'd never see the light of day with Lily this side of Christmas.

At last she withdrew those tender, hot hands, which shouldn't be allowed out, especially at work. 'As long as you're all right.'

'Serves him right for gulping his food.' Devlin laughed on his way out of the room.

She hadn't cared they weren't alone when she'd banged his back, pressed her fingers into his muscles. 'Want a glass of water?' Lily asked.

Did she not have a clue she'd just tipped him

on his head? Looking at her, he knew she did. There was a glint of humour in those potent eyes, and the corners of her lush mouth kept lifting. 'Yes, with lots of ice.' He'd probably choke on a cube, but he needed her to look away for a few moments while he gathered some sense and got back to normal.

Except normal with Lily as he'd known it had flown the coop. Picking up his lunch, he tried for a third time to get some of it down where it was needed, and succeeded this time.

'Here.' Lily plonked a brimming glass in front of him and sat down again. 'You have a busy morning?'

He nodded. 'Seems half of Remuera's come down with the flu over the weekend.' Hopefully those patients he'd seen would keep their bugs to themselves. 'It's the last thing I want.'

'Did you have the flu jab?'

Duh. He should have remembered that. 'Yes, I did. It's offered to anyone who's had cancer in the past five years.' Now he was mentioning his illness, something he never did, especially around work. Thank goodness the staffroom was unusually quiet. 'Where is everyone?'

'We're both running late. Also Joanne and Suzie went down to the shops. There's a sale on at Petal's. I'd have joined them if I hadn't been running behind in my schedule.'

'I take it that's a women's clothing store.'

'Not just any store. One of the best.' She grinned. 'My favourite. Classy, beautiful outfits any woman would give her eye teeth for.'

'Or a small fortune.'

Lily laughed. 'Got you.'

'You'll keep,' he growled. She'd been winding him up. That's exactly what he'd said to her once before, only that time she'd given him a blast about not being ashamed of her comfortable lifestyle. He'd been rude, but she'd seemed to relish not having to worry about how to fund her way through med school. Now he knew better.

That camp at Whangaparaoa would've put a massive hole in her bank account, and no doubt continued to do so. 'Is there an annual fundraising event to put money into the camp coffers?' He hadn't found anything online about how other finances were raised.

Lily glanced around the empty room, as though checking no one had sneaked in while they'd been talking. 'No, and it's not necessary. It may become so in the future, but for now everything's under control.'

'You take donations, though?'

'The board accepts them. I hope we never have to go public on fundraising. There are so many necessary charitable causes out there, I don't want to add to the growing list. There's not enough money to go around as it is.'

'Anyone ever told you that you have a big heart, Lily?' She really did. Sure, she wasn't the only person out there supporting those in need, but he liked it that Lily did. It made her even more special. Made his hands tingle with warmth.

Picking up her sandwich, she took a bite, and chewed thoughtfully. He guessed she wasn't going to answer.

Max followed her example, finally managing to eat his lunch without further discomfort. The silence between them turned comfortable. Until Lily stood up and he got an eyeful of a perfectly curved backside in fitted trousers as she crossed to the sink. At least he'd finished eating. And drinking the ice-cold water. But his heart pounded while his mouth dried. Snatching the paper bag, he screwed it up, threw it at the bin, and stood up. 'I'll see you later.'

He had things to think about before he made a move in any direction. Her need for a baby. His growing need to father one. What would she say if he offered to be the donor? Unless he got over his concerns about the future, she wasn't going to get the opportunity to consider the idea.

He was halfway to his office when he heard her calling after him.

'Max, wait a minute.'

He watched her every step, the gentle, *sexy* swing of her hips, the light shining in her eyes as she focused on him. What was this about?

'Have dinner with me tonight?' she asked as she reached him.

As he drew a breath, he was zapped with a fragrance that was all Lily and nothing like the chemical air of the medical centre. 'I'd li—' No, try again. Be sensible. 'Sorry, but I'm busy. All week.'

Annoyance, even anger sliced through him from those now not so shiny eyes. 'Just because you've pulled the plug on what we started last week, it doesn't mean we can't be friendly and spend some time together.'

'You think that's wise? Given where we were when I…' he flipped his fingers in the air '…pulled the plug? On a few kisses?'

Her throat moved upwards as she swallowed hard. 'I like how we've been getting along on other levels.'

Her disappointment made him feel like a heel for being so blunt. But how could he sit across from her in a restaurant and pretend he didn't want to take her to bed? Or deny he was considering having a baby with her? Or ignore she was giving his heart a damned hard shove in the direction he'd sworn off ever going?

'Lily—' Give her a break. She'd only said what he thought. 'True.' Could he do this? Without going completely bonkers? He gave in. 'I can't have dinner with you tonight, I do genuinely have something on. How about Thursday night? You'll have done four days here and can download on me if you need to. And...' he held his hand up as she started to say something '...we can continue getting to know each other and enjoying ourselves.' There was merit in that. He'd be able to think some more about the baby idea. Why? Lily would be his pick if he wanted someone to have his children. The only question he had to ask himself was if he truly wanted to do this. It meant putting his fears aside, but in reality they'd been lessening since he'd met up with Lily again. 'So, are you available Thursday night?'

The twinkle was back. The smallest of smiles, too. Which meant so was the heat in his aching gut. 'I'll make sure I am.'

Relief swamped his chest. 'Talk more before then.' He turned away before he came up with other reasons to stand talking in the hallway when he had patients waiting.

CHAPTER NINE

'THE VIEW'S STUNNING.' Max was standing with his hands in his pockets on the small deck, looking out towards the Harbour Bridge with all its lights.

Lily stood beside him. 'During the day, seeing the boats in the marina is pretty too. Being on the lower level, I have a back yard as well, which I'm going to make into an outdoor entertaining area.'

'Any trees to cut down?'

She laughed. 'I don't think the neighbours would be very friendly if I started up my saw.' Her elbows dug into her sides and she did a little dance internally. Max was with her, in her home, and it felt right.

He turned just then and placed his hands on her shoulders. 'I know I said no to furthering our relationship, but I'm not doing a great job of staying away from you.' Bright eyes locked on hers. 'I have to kiss you.'

Yes. Up on her toes, she leaned in and placed her lips on his before he could retract his words. *Yes.* Wow. His mouth opened, and his tongue explored hers, tasting her, driving her to the brink so fast her knees were knocking. Wrapping her arms around his waist she held on tight, and kissed him back, again and again.

A sharp, chilly gust of wind slammed into them.

Max lifted his head. 'Inside?'

Lily pulled him and slid the door shut. And returned to his arms, his mouth, pressing up so that her hard peaks ached against his chest.

'Max?' she whispered. They couldn't stop now. Her whole body was rippling with desire, the sparks he brought on with a smile were now burning out of control.

He leaned back, his arms still around her waist. Then he shoved one hand through his hair, staring at her as though he couldn't get enough. He leaned down to kiss her forehead.

He'd changed his mind. He was leaving. This was goodnight. She held her breath, begging silently for him to stay.

'Hell.' Swinging her up into his arms, he asked, 'Where's your bedroom?'

Nodding towards the door on the right, she buried her face in his neck, breathing him in, soaking up his heat, absorbing the heat from his hands on her thigh and back. *Yes.* Max was with her. She'd make the most of tonight and wait to see what followed.

It wasn't enough to be held against him. Her lips sought his mouth, tasting, touching, soaking him up. Her body reacted instantly, the heat and desire returning in a flood, softening some places, tightening others. Blinding all reason, drowning any warnings from the sane side of her brain. She wanted Max. Had done so since first seeing him again. It was something she needed to do, to have, to share. But she couldn't bear it if they stopped this time. 'Max?' she squeaked around the rock of need blocking her throat. So much for not getting close.

'Max?' He'd heard his name between their mouths. Drawn out and filled with hunger. Sexy beyond measure. She could not be wanting him to haul on the brakes. But he wouldn't continue if she didn't want to. Lifting his mouth away, feeling the loss instantly, he locked his eyes on those green ones so close. 'Yes?'

'I want you.'

Relief poured through him. Then it stopped. 'Lily, I can't promise anything more.' But he wanted to, more than ever.

Stiffening, she leaned back in his arms. 'I

understand, and I say to hell with that. It's one night, Max. One step. Let's see where it leads.'

Those alluring eyes dragged him into her understanding and longing. 'Are you sure?' Because he was falling, falling into her, into the emotions he hadn't had for so long. One night? Was that even possible? But walking away now wasn't either.

'Absolutely.'

In one movement their clothes were torn off. Lily held his hands as she sprawled across the bed, pulling him with her. Covering her with his roused body, his mouth trailed kisses over any skin he could reach. Lily bucked beneath him. Her lips covered one nipple, her tongue flicking back and forth, hot and sharp, driving him to the edge. 'Slow down,' he gasped against her stomach. He wanted to pleasure Lily first, only it had to be fast because he was near breaking point.

'Can't. Don't want to.'

Phew. Reaching between them, he found her throbbing need.

Instantly she was pushing up into him. 'Now. *Max.*'

As she cried out his name he lifted up and entered her heat.

She climaxed immediately, pulling him to join her straightaway.

Her body was his, hers. They were together and he never wanted this to end.

It seemed for ever before he was breathing anywhere near normally. Lying on his back, Lily sprawled along his body, the rate of her breasts rising and falling slowing down, he knew nothing but happiness. It had been fast and amazing. It had been what he'd needed, and had hoped for since coming face to face with Lily for the first time again after all he'd been through. 'I know I've said it before, but I've really missed you.' Staying away from love might be the worst choice to make.

Lily jerked against him. 'What? Did I hear right?'

Did I really say that? He had, and now an explanation was required. If possible. Lily wouldn't let it go. Why did he feel he'd missed her? Because she hadn't bowed to what he'd wanted, had expected to get as good as she got, and while that had bruised his ego it had also made him enjoy her. He'd never forgotten a moment of their fling, whereas other women had come and gone and he struggled to recall very much about them. It wasn't something he was proud of, but there was no getting away from it. 'Nothing wrong with your hearing but, then, we are entwined.'

'Very funny.'

He tugged her sideways and pulled her over his body. His hands slipped under her jersey and found her full, warm breasts. Pushing the jersey up, he covered one nipple with his mouth and tongued her until she writhed with need. For him.

Then Lily's hands caressed, stroking him. Blocking his mind to everything but her body, her fingers, those lips. Lily.

Together they left talk behind and rose on a wave of passion that shook Max to the core, had him wondering how he was ever going to be able to call a halt to this second fling with the most amazing woman he'd had the luck to get to know in bed. And out of it.

Max laughed as he ran around a gathering of people waiting for the Saturday market to open. The air was crisp and smelled of fruit from the stalls just inside the gate. His head was light, his body bursting with energy, and even his stomach had given the aches a miss. He was happy.

Lily had kicked him out of her bed just after the sun had peeped in around the curtains. She was heading to the farm to spend the day with the family. She would miss the first breakfast because he'd fallen back into bed and tucked her under him to make love again. Making love was so much more special than having sex. Care was involved, love, laughter, sharing.

He'd been utterly bonkers to think he could walk away. There was nothing wrong with a little bit of madness. It added to the fun. Life was good. Lily was his heart's desire. And brought on a whole lot more longing just by standing in front of him or touching his arm with one of those perfectly manicured fingers or smiling mischievously.

Beyond the market he picked up his pace. After last night's time with Lily his body ached in places he'd forgotten were there and he felt good. He loved her. It was hard to believe when he'd stuck to his determination not to get into a relationship for so long. He had sure dropped that fast. Too fast? Would it come back to bite him? If it did, he'd get up again. Lily gave him the confidence to let go the fears that had charted his life for too long. He was strong, had survived a bumpy childhood, and did have love to share.

Could he do this? Really? When he'd always been motivated to save his heart? He could still hurt Lily, be hurt himself. So far he only knew Lily was happy to spend time with him. He had no idea what she felt beyond that. She was always willing to spend time together, had said she wasn't ready to say goodbye, but did that mean she might eventually love him?

Jogging on the spot while waiting for the pedestrian crossing buzzer to go, he shook his head. He'd just have to make the most of the time they had together and see where it led.

He could use the time to think hard about whether to offer her the chance to have the baby she so longed for.

He tripped, straightened, walked across the road and into the park beyond. Sure, the idea had crossed his mind often, but he hadn't really believed he was serious. Was he now? Was this just so Lily could have a child, or was he beginning to accept he could be a parent? If that was the case, he'd want to marry Lily, have a proper family.

I'm getting way ahead of myself.

This needed time to get right. But it was starting to feel perfect, as though he'd found his reason for being, which always came back to Lily.

Lily tried to pay for dinner.

Max refused to let her. 'I like spoiling you and intend to do it often.' His eyes slid to the gorgeous woman walking at his side towards his car, which was parked outside the restaurant. Yes, damn it, he wanted Lily. In his life, at his side; sharing the future, parenthood, *everything.*

She was looking up at him with a cheeky smile and those big eyes sparkling as though the sun was behind them. 'I'm allowed to spoil you, too.'

As he pulled out into the traffic, he said, 'One day I'll let you.' He was having too much fun giving to Lily. Four weeks of time spent together, both in bed and out of it, and he'd done a complete about-face. To the point of falling in love. He loved Lily, no ifs or buts. He completely accepted it. They shared meals at their homes or in restaurants, they talked and laughed, and made love.

'We've just sat through a green,' said the woman screwing with his head. And obviously with his ability to see green when it was right in front of him.

'Thought I heard some tooting.' Speeding away, he tried to laugh. It came out sharp and not at all funny. This was serious. For a moment the old fear of getting too involved popped up. But either he was or he wasn't. Which would it be? Having accepted he loved Lily, it meant there was only one way to go. He had to admit it. He was already on the way to a full-on relationship with her. She appeared just as eager. So when would the questions stop bothering him?

Lily leaned close, scrutinising him. 'Are you all right? You suddenly looked exhausted.'

Right on cue, he yawned. 'I am feeling a bit tired.' Shattered best described the way his aching body struggled to remain upright and his head to think clearly. That might be why he had all those blasted questions trotting around his skull. He'd been fighting exhaustion all day. 'I did nearly suggest another night for dinner, but I didn't want to miss seeing you.'

Lily gasped. 'Did I hear right?' She smiled briefly, before surprising him. 'Max, we are getting on really well, aren't we?'

That sounded like she had some doubts. About her feelings? Or his? 'I think we're doing fine.'

'That's a relief. For a moment there you sounded strained.'

'Probably because I hardly slept a wink last night.' Too busy thinking about Lily.

'As long as you're not coming down with something. That flu's still knocking people over all around the city.'

'It's a nasty one this year. Affecting the elderly the worst, though.' He'd better not be getting it. One, he'd spent enough time being unwell to last for ever. Two, it was busy at work with staff away with the flu. But his head was beginning to pound. 'Don't worry about me. I'm fine.'

Lily gave him one her heart-twisting smiles

as he pulled up outside the apartment block. 'You want to come up for a celebratory coffee? Or drink?'

Of course he did. But he wouldn't be much fun. 'I'd love to but I'm going home to take some pills and get some sleep. Do you mind?'

'No.' She smiled. 'It's fine, truly. You look terrible and sleep is probably the best remedy.' She leaned in to kiss him and he turned his head so her lips caressed his cheek. The smile slowly faded. Placing her hand on the door handle, she said, 'I'll see you tomorrow. Sleep well.' And she was out and closing the door behind her.

Damn it. He hadn't wanted to give her whatever was ailing him. He should race after her and explain, but that would take too much energy, and energy seemed to be rapidly disappearing. He'd phone when he got home. He waited until Lily had let herself in and the front entrance door clipped shut behind her. Another yawn dragged at his body as he pulled away from the kerb. There would be plenty of time for talking later.

In the morning Max groaned as he tried to roll over. The pain was crippling. Eventually he crawled out of bed and under the hot shower, his head feeling as though it would explode any moment. Every muscle in his body ached, and there was a dull pain in his gut. Near where the tumour had been removed.

Nausea soared. He leapt out of the shower to sit down, head on his knees, until the feeling passed. No bloody way. Not now. Now when he was getting his life in order. Not when he'd decided to love Lily. It couldn't have come back. There'd been no warning signs. As if there had been the first time.

He'd been too busy being happy with Lily to notice any minor health problems. Thinking back over the weeks, he realised the tiredness wasn't new, had been growing for some time, and the ache in his gut was real. It wasn't psychosomatic. Prodding with his fingers he couldn't find anything out of the ordinary but, then, a tumour wasn't that easy to find.

Pulling himself upright, he dried off and picked up the razor to shave for the day, aiming for normality. He was overreacting. If anything, he had the flu. This was a hypochondriac's reaction, and he wasn't one of those. But what if…?

Stop it. Get on with the day.

His hand was shaking, and by the time he'd removed his whiskers there were two nicks on his chin. If this was flu he had no right to go into work and spread it further. Great. He could stay at home and talk himself into any illness he liked. Wrapping himself in the thick, navy bathrobe that had been hanging on the back of the bathroom door, he went into his bedroom and sank down on the bed, all energy gone, and swallowed some more headache pills and half a glass of water, and stared at the floor between his feet. Just a few minutes and the pills would kick in and he could get up and ring Devlin about tests to make sure the cancer hadn't returned. Because his gut was saying it had.

The phone ringing on his bedside table woke Max. The time showed nine ten. As he snatched up the phone he leapt out of bed and slammed his hand against the wall to prevent crashing to the floor. His head was going round and round, his legs barely held him upright. Sinking onto the edge of the bed, he pressed the phone icon. 'Hello, Lily.'

Lily. Darling Lily. He had to call it off with her. This was the wake-up call he needed to make him see sense. He could not get serious with her, couldn't marry her and have children together. Tears streamed down his cheeks and he let them fall onto his chest.

'Max? Are you all right? Where are you? The office tried ringing you, then Devlin. You haven't had an accident, have you?' Lily sounded frantic, full of concern.

Well, she would, wouldn't she? His heart

warmed, and for a moment he dared to dream,
then his stomach squeezed painfully, shatter-
ing the hope. He snapped, 'I'm fine.' Glancing
at the phone, he saw what he hadn't noticed before. Three missed phone calls. 'I was asleep.'

'Max, you were tired last night. Have you got
the flu despite having the vaccination? Or something else? Food poisoning from those scampi?'

That possibility had never crossed his mind
and the symptoms didn't stack up anyway. 'Not
food poisoning. Possibly the flu. I slept all night
after downing some pills, and have just taken
some more.' Say anything to keep her from asking too many questions. He was going to hurt
her but he'd prefer to be on his feet when he
did that.

'Stay in bed. Janice is back, Andrew's called
in sick. The medical centre's not immune.'

'If I don't come in you'll all be a lot busier.'
Shut up. There was no way he could stand up
for more than a few minutes. Trying to work
with patients was definitely out.

'Then we'll be at risk of catching whatever
you've got. I'll get you a prescription for the tab-
lets we're all prescribing and drop them off at
lunchtime. If you're really nice, I'll bring some
lunch to go with them.'

The thought of food didn't do him any favours
but there was a remote possibility he might feel

a bit better in a few hours. 'The spare key is in the peg basket attached to the washing line around the back.'

'Anything else you need?' Lily asked.

'No. Thanks.'

'Right. I'll see you later. And, Max? Don't spend the morning stressing about what's wrong with you. It doesn't help, and will only prevent you getting much-needed sleep.' She hung up.

'Yes, Doctor.' As he dropped back against the pillows and tugged the duvet up to his chin, he wanted to shout at the world for doing this to him. Not now, not when Lily read him too well, and he liked that. She understood he'd be worried sick about what was ailing him. She wouldn't laugh at him, but she'd sure as hell make sure he didn't spend his time carrying on like a hypochondriac. She also wasn't going to be happy when he told her they really were over this time. Because he had to. For her sake.

Damn it, he was medically trained, knew about symptoms, and understood how some people could overthink their situation until they made themselves ill. Not once had he ever thought he'd be one of those, and yet here he was, acting stupidly. The fear was back, ramping up fast. If only the cancer hadn't returned. That's all he asked. Not when he'd finally decided to make a go of the future, to stop worrying about letting others down. Was the fact he'd taken a step towards a future with Lily putting him in his place for hoping for too much?

Coming back into his life, Lily had tossed all his post-cancer beliefs out the window like they didn't mean a thing. She'd woken him up so that for the first time ever he wanted a permanent relationship, to be married to the woman he loved, and to have a family. He wanted to love and be loved, and he was halfway there, so now all he would've had to do was make her fall in love with him. But not any more. He was backing off.

First he'd ring Devlin. The man was his GP, and a friend, and understood his fears.

'Hey, how're you doing?' Lily leaned against the doorframe of Max's bedroom and took a good, long at him. Dark shadows stained his upper cheeks, while traces of red filled the lower half of his face. His eyes were spewing exhaustion. 'Looks as though you've got yourself a fever.'

'The sheets and pillows are soaked.' He shuffled up the bed to lean back against the headboard, looking everywhere but at her. Like she wasn't welcome.

She'd ignore that for now. Devlin said Max had called for a prescription, when she'd said she get him what he required. That had stung, but there was no point in making a mountain out of it. 'Don't go getting cold. I'll take your temperature then put the kettle on if you want a hot drink.' She got the thermometer out of the medical bag she carried and moved across to the bed.

Max obliged by turning his head to show his ear. 'This is crazy.'

She managed a laugh. 'It sure is. But it shows you're human. The flu's doing the rounds of the medical centre.' She read the scanner. 'Slightly high. To be expected.'

'You be careful. Don't want you getting sick.' His smile was lopsided, and a little sad.

Punching him lightly in the arm, she shook her head. 'I'm tough. I'll be fine. Right, what do you want to drink? I've brought sandwiches and a sweet muffin for your lunch.'

'Hot water will do. Not sure I want to eat.'

'Too bad.' She got him a large mug of hot water and a plate with two sandwiches. Then she got a mug of coffee and some sandwiches for herself and went to sit on the end of the bed. 'Did you go back to sleep after I rang?'

'Hard not to, exhaustion being the theme of the day.'

Talk about cranky. 'Most patients I've seen with this flu say the same. It takes up to a week to be back on your feet,' she warned.

'Me lying around that long? I don't think so.'

'Get over yourself. This week you're a patient, not a doctor. Now, tell me what other symptoms you're getting, real or not.' She'd known the moment he'd talked to her that morning that he'd been worrying the cancer was back. It had been in his hesitancy and the strain deepening his voice. So unlike the confident Max she knew.

He glared at her.

She laughed back, refusing to show concern for his fears. That would only endorse them, and he didn't need that, though she did sympathise. 'Come on.'

'Lily.' He stopped, swallowed and stared towards the window.

Her heart slowed dangerously. This wasn't about her helping him. This was about them. Deep inside, pain was already growing. Now she recognised the look in his face. Regret. Sorrow. And that damned determination. 'Don't.'

'I have to. I was wrong to think I could have a future without upsetting you. Or me.' Those khaki eyes locked on her. 'I'm sorry. I've let us both down. Please, don't waste your time trying to convince me otherwise. I'd like you to leave now, and only be in contact at work.' His voice cracked, and a lone tear rolled down his cheek. 'I'm doing this for you, Lily.'

Her heart stopped completely. Her hands were

wet. Her stomach so tight a golf ball would be large beside it. He couldn't do this without fighting for them. Max was afraid of being hurt, of hurting her. Well, he was already hurting, so was she. But the only way to get through to him was to show him, not tell him. It was going to take time. 'When did you last have a colonoscopy?'

'Don't do this, Lily.'

'Answer the question, will you?' She could do tough if it meant winning him over.

His sigh hung between them. 'Twelve months ago. I was having severe stomach pains. Turned out it was a false alarm.'

Bet he'd panicked then, too. 'You've had your share of medical dramas, Max.'

'I'm not afraid of getting sick or having surgery. It's the unknown I hate, especially when it comes to the people I hold dear.'

Sitting on the edge of the bed, she reached for his hand.

Max pulled away. 'Please, go back to work. I don't need you here.'

Low blow. But she was better than that. 'I get why you're worried, but I truly believe you've got the flu and nothing more. Your stomach could be aching because you're so worried, or because of that dinner you ate last night, or from fear about the future.'

'You might be right. I might be overreacting. But what if I'm right? I don't want you nursing me through it, being stuck with me no matter what. I care deeply for you, Lily, and that's why I have to let you go.'

Her head was shaking from side to side. She couldn't stand, she'd fall flat on her face. Her skin was cold, her heart hot and thumping. He cared deeply? Did that mean he loved her? Then he had just set himself up for a battle, and he was going to lose. 'Right.' Her forehead pulled tight as she arched one eyebrow. 'I hear you. Now I'm out of here.' For now. 'The waiting room opens again in fifteen.'

She'd reached the door when he spoke.

'Lily, I am so sorry.'

Gripping the doorframe to prevent herself rushing over and hugging him tight, she forced herself to smile and said, 'One step at a time, Max. Let's find out what's wrong first, shall we?'

'No, not we. Devlin's helping me. Don't come back here. I'll see you when I return to work.' His voice broke and he turned to stare at the window.

Which was good because then he didn't see the stream of tears pouring down her face, leaving lines in her make-up. 'Bye, Max.' But not goodbye. She had his key. He needed food, and to be looked out for, and love. And there was plenty of that for him in her heart.

The afternoon dragged. More cases of flu, a referral to a cardiology department, a malaria recurrence, and the removal of sun damage by minor surgery kept Lily busy, and yet the minutes crept by.

'I saw Max at lunchtime,' she told Devlin when they had finally closed the doors and were having a coffee in his office.

'Thought you might've. How is he?'

'Physically or mentally?' If only she could bite her nails to relieve some of the tension holding her in a twist. She loved Max and he'd told her to get out of his life. 'He's a mess. I believe he's got the flu. He doesn't.'

'What about the stomach-ache he's been having?'

'Stress? Exhaustion?' She lifted one shoulder, let it drop. 'I—I don't know.'

'Neither do I, but I think you're right, it's flu.'

Lily waited but when Devlin remained quiet, her tongue got the better of her. 'He's so negative about his future. He doesn't want to love someone and then let them down by getting ill again. He doesn't want to take risks.' Only to Devlin could she talk about this.

He was watching her with something much too like sympathy in his expression.

A look she wasn't grateful for. 'I am going to fight him on this.'

'No surprise there.' Devlin paused, seemed to be collecting his thoughts. 'The problem is that Max is susceptible to overthinking his health when it's not perfect. Something many people who've had cancer go through. You have to wait this out, Lily.'

She lifted her head to look at the man who was like a second father. Her stomach rolled over. *He knew.* Knew she loved Max. Knew how hard she'd fight for him. 'Really?'

'First, he isn't your patient. Second, he's not going to allow you to stand with him while he waits to find out what's going on.' He began tapping at his keyboard.

'You can't tell me anything.' She accepted that. But, 'Are there any times I should be blocking out patient appointments over the coming days because of other commitments?'

'Like I said, I can't tell you anything. Now I think it's time we went home and relaxed after the hectic day we've all had.' He stood up and winked. 'Close my computer down for me, will you? I've got a call to make.'

After Devlin left his office, Lily stepped around his desk and read the screen in front of her. Max had an appointment for a CT scan at seven tomorrow and Declan had also ordered a CRP and a full blood count.

She sighed. The CT scan was the best scan for the condition, and there were nearly twenty-five hours before that was done. She'd have to be patient. But she could help Max in the meantime. He'd need dinner in some form, and there'd been little in his fridge or pantry that would be of any use. She'd hit the supermarket then deliver to his bedside.

He could say what he liked but she wasn't disappearing out of his life yet. If at all.

'I told you to stay away, Lily,' Max snapped, when he opened his front door to the strident rings that had gone on and on. He'd thought the taxi he'd ordered to take him to the radiology department at Auckland Central Hospital had got the time wrong. Bloody woman. It was hard enough knowing he'd kicked her out of his life, then finding food parcels in his fridge, without having her turning up on his doorstep and waving car keys in his face.

'Stop being a grump. I'm giving you a ride to your appointment, that's all. Nothing out of the ordinary for friends.' Her smile was small but genuine. She wasn't letting him off the hook.

Did he have to get mean and nasty to make

what he'd said about their relationship sink in? 'There are taxis in this city. I have one coming in twenty minutes.'

'Then you'll have to cancel it. I'm taking you there and back. It will be quicker and more comfortable.'

How? The temperature outside was freezing. 'Oh, for goodness' sake, come inside.' Max stepped back, holding the door wide, slamming it shut the moment Lily stepped past him. 'This isn't going to get you anywhere, Lily. I meant what I said.'

She shrugged and carried on walking towards his lounge. 'I know you did.'

'So why are you here?'

She sat down on the couch and looked up at him. 'I love you, Max, and I won't give up on you because you are afraid of hurting me. I'm tough, I can take it. I will take it because I believe you care about me, too.'

He swallowed the bile that rose in his mouth. Lily loved him. He'd been hoping for that before the thought of being ill again had recurred. She loved him and he'd hurt her already. 'I…' He stopped. What could he say to make any of this better?

'I mean it. I love you, and that means whatever the outcome of your CT is, I'm here for you. I won't go away just because I'm hurting for you. Hurting for us. I am going to be there when you find out, and I'm going to be here for ever.'

His knees gave out and his butt hit the edge of the chair behind him. Gripping the edges, he pushed back onto it. 'You don't know what you're saying, what you're letting yourself in for.'

'Oh, yes, I do.' Lily stood up, and held out her hand. 'Come on. Let's go find out what's going on.'

CHAPTER TEN

LILY SAT RIGID on the plastic chair in the waiting room, barely daring to breathe.

Max had been gone ages. CTs didn't take this long. What was going on? Had they found a tumour? If that was the case, why hadn't he asked for her to join him while the doctor discussed it? Had he gone out another door to get away from facing up to her with the horrific news?

'Lily?' A pair of familiar, jeans-clad legs appeared in her line of sight.

Deep breath. Her hands clenched.

'Lily, look at me.'

Slowly raising her head, she found Max's gaze on her and a small smile on his lips. 'Tell me.'

'No tumour.'

'Truly?' He wouldn't be smiling if there was.

'Truly.' He reached a hand out. 'Take me home?'

Home. 'Meaning?'

His smile faded.

So did the glimmer of hope that had begun to rise in her heart. 'I see.' Ignoring his hand, she pushed off the chair and headed for the door. 'Come on.'

It was a silent trip home. Silent and tense. When she pulled up in his driveway she said, 'I'm coming in for a coffee.'

'Don't do this to yourself, Lily.'

She shoved her door open and got out, waited impatiently for Max to do the same before pinging the lock.

Once inside she put the coffee on as though it was her place to do so. 'Sit down before you fall down.' He mightn't have cancer, but that flu was punishing him. And *she* hadn't started on him yet.

When the coffee was ready and they were sitting at the table with a mug each, Lily drew a deep breath and reminded herself why she wasn't giving up. She loved Max and would do anything for him. As well as making him get over the past and move on, even if it didn't include her. 'You are letting yourself down, Max.'

'You think so?'

'Come on. Haven't we been great together these past weeks? Think about the times we've spent talking and laughing, enjoying meals, being a couple.'

'I have thought of exactly the same things.'

'You were happy with me? You did start looking forward to a future you'd hidden from yourself?'

'Ye-es.'

'Then think about the camp. About those kids and how each and every one of them got up after being knocked down physically or mentally to carry on. How they wouldn't let anything keep them from trying for what they want.' Her hands shook too much to lift the mug so she gripped them together in her lap. 'Didn't they show you anything?'

Max reached across to touch her arm. 'Hope. Strength. Love for life.'

'Where's yours, Max?'

'Lily, you don't understand how it hurts me to hurt you.'

'You're saying you love me?' Thump, thump. Please mean that. Please.

'I'm saying we're over.'

Lily sagged forward. *Here I go again. What's so wrong with me that men don't stay around?*

Pain bashed at her. She loved him. So much so she'd begun to feel he might just be starting to reciprocate her feelings. And he'd pulled the plug. Did that mean he didn't care for her? Or that he did and was afraid to follow through? Wasn't that idea just her being overly hopeful?

When she'd already been here and knew the outcome? No, not this time. She wasn't accepting this. Not yet. Not so quickly or easily. But first she had to get away, think it through, not react blindly to a past pain. Not let this man walk away without a fight because others had done that.

Her face had blanched. Her eyes were dark with sadness and, yes, anger.

Max felt sick to his toes. But how else did he get through to her?

Silence stretched between them.

Finally he had to fill it. 'You've got nothing to say, have you?' Pain lashed at his heart. He did not want Lily to walk away, yet she had to.

'Until you start accepting you have a rosy future if you're brave enough to grab it with both hands and make the most of it, you are going to be unhappy.' With that, she walked out of his house, quietly snicking the lock shut behind her.

Leaving him aching to hold her, desperate for them to be together, sharing the night in his bed. His lonely bed, where he now headed after swallowing a handful of painkillers.

The house creaked, highlighting his aloneness. No, damn it. Loneliness. For the first time in his adult life he missed the company of someone in his house as they went about everyday things. While he lay in bed and then got up to eat and return to the warmth of his duvet. There were the days Lily had arrived with prepared meals, talked with him, laughed over stupid stories of his or her past, discussed what they both hoped for in their futures at the medical hub. It had been real and fun, honest and hopeful.

Now she'd walked out without kissing him, without a speech about drinking lots of water and taking his pills.

He mustn't forget this was Lily Scott. She'd changed, but there was no denying she was still that strong, independent woman who always followed her own heart, looking out for others along the way. Like Josie. Putting her niece's needs before her own. He'd seen her do the same with patients, years ago and recently.

Lily had put him first since he'd come down with the flu. She'd seen through his fear and basically, kindly, told him to get over it. He'd been given a second chance and he was wasting it. His words, her meaning.

His heart thumped once, hard and painfully. Lily Scott. Since his first day on duty as a junior doctor in Auckland Central Hospital's emergency department she'd been a thorn in his side. Annoying, frustrating, aloof, sexy and tormenting. And a hundred other things. He'd thought he'd forgotten her when she'd left the department, but in reality he never had. She'd been there, under the surface, leaping up into his consciousness the moment he'd heard her name and realised they were going to work at the same clinic. With that came the memories. Bad, great and everything in between.

Lily was in his psyche. Like it or not. Like? Try love. Yeah, he'd gone and fallen head over feet in love with Lily. He had a choice to make. He'd done it earlier then backed off in a flaming hurry. This time he had to be one hundred percent certain. Did he take a chance on the future he'd been handed by the specialists and his own determination to survive, and declare his love to her, ask for a life together, share the raising of their child, children even? Or...his chest rose then fell...move away out of her life and that of her baby that she'd have and adore for ever?

A sour taste came to his mouth. He couldn't do that. Not without trying to convince her he was worthy of her, and would stick with her through whatever the future threw at them. The good and the not so good. Even if... Another long breath. Even if the cancer returned and wreaked havoc on him. Them. They were both strong, together they'd be resilient. They'd have a rock-solid, loving relationship.

Was he ready to commit to life with Lily? Regardless of how she felt about him, he had to be certain this love was for real, for ever, before he did anything about it.

'Make an appointment to see me in a week's time,' Max told his patient. 'I want to see how you're coping with the new diet regime.' The middle-aged woman had a fasting glucose of ten mmol/L.

'I started the day you phoned to say my blood result was indicative of diabetes. I'm walking every day.'

'That's good, Meryl, but I'd like to keep an eye on you until you're used to the new routine. Any time you're uncertain about anything you can talk to our nurses, too. I've seen patients start out well then falter after the tedium sets in. This is a life-changer, not something you do for a few weeks.'

'I understand. I have been reading about diabetes and how other people manage. It's a bit scary.' She stood up and headed for the door. 'I'll make an appointment when I pay for today.'

Max headed out to the waiting room. 'Bill, come in.' He watched as his sixty-five-year-old patient limped across the room. 'That hip's getting worse. I'm going to refer you to an orthopaedic surgeon,' he said as Bill settled onto a chair by his desk.

'It's still good enough. I get around fine. I

only came for a repeat prescription of the anti-inflammatory.'

Max shook his head. Stubborn old guy. 'Get up on the bed so I can check that hip out thoroughly.'

Bill dropped his jeans, hobbled over to the bed and hauled himself onto it to lie down. 'I'm still mowing the lawns, going to the gym and riding my cycle to work.'

'From one to ten, ten being the highest, what's the pain level now?'

'Five…six.'

Max didn't believe him. Pain had reflected out of his eyes as he'd stood up from the chair. 'When you ride to work?'

Bill sighed. 'Eight. On a good day.'

'Lie on your good side, please.' Max lifted Bill's leg with the damaged hip and watched Bill's face for a reaction. He didn't move it far. 'Now I'm going to rotate your leg gently. Tell me if it's too painful.'

'You can stop before you start,' Bill grunted. 'You win. How long do I have to wait for an op?'

'That'll be up to the surgeon and whether you go private or public.'

'I've got health insurance so I won't have to hang about on the public list.'

'Good. You can get up.' He wasn't going to inflict any more discomfort on him. Bill knew as well as he did that hip needed to be replaced sooner rather than later. 'I'll refer you to one of the surgeons next door, unless you have a preference.'

'You know best, Max.' Bill gasped as he shoved his bad leg into his jeans.

'That's settled, then. I'll write a prescription, too. Anything else you need to talk about?' Max brought up the correct screen.

'No, I'm good to go. You've given me enough of a shock already.'

'You really weren't thinking the time for surgery was close?'

'I was hoping it wasn't. I get around all right. There are people far worse off than me who aren't getting their hips done.' Bill looked baffled.

'I can't answer for them, though I know you seriously need to have this done. You won't know yourself afterwards and will wonder why you waited so long.' Scrawling his signature on the prescription printout, he handed it to his patient. 'I'll get that referral away today. And go easy on the bike. It wouldn't help to fall off and damage that hip any further.'

Bill ignored that, pocketed his script and headed for the door. 'Thanks, Max. I'll be seeing you.'

Leaning back in his chair, Max flicked a

pen back and forth between his fingers. Bill had been his last patient for the day. For the week. Damn, he was tired. The flu had done its number on him, but this past week had been more about lack of sleep. About thinking about Lily and how impossible it would be to carry on without her in his life, at his side. In other words, he was a fool to deny himself love and a happy future. Lily made him happy, made him look at his choices differently and want to change them so he could have that future—with her. He did love her, every little and big thing about her. The future looked bleak without her in it. *Would she have him now?* The big question that kept him awake too much. There was only one way to find out.

'You staying there, daydreaming, all night?' Devlin asked from the doorway. 'Or are you joining the rest of us for a drink?'

'Neither. I'm heading home. There are things I need to do.'

'Like talk to Lily.'

Max's head snapped up and he stared at Devlin. 'Lily?'

'Yes, the woman you've been doing your best to avoid and when you can't avoid her have been friendly with in an offhand manner.'

'I was that obvious?' What did Lily think after all she'd done for him when he'd been ill?

'I've known Lily most of her life. I can read her well and she's confused about you.'

Ouch. That hurt. 'I see.'

'Do you?' Devlin was sounding like a father figure, not the medical hub's boss. 'If so, then fix what's holding you both back from being happy.'

Pushing up from his chair, Max picked up his jacket and bag. 'I intend to.'

Lily wasn't at her apartment when Max got there. She wasn't there an hour later when he tried again, driving through a torrential downpour that had flooded roads, with his windscreen wipers unable to cope. When he finally made it back home she wasn't answering her phone either. She could be anywhere, but he suspected he knew exactly where she'd gone.

It was too dangerous to drive far at the moment. He could only hope that Lily had reached Whangaparaoa before the weather bomb hit. Or it had given that area a miss. He'd take to the road at first light.

The weather had played havoc with the roads and maintenance crews were out in force, causing traffic delays that had Max's blood fizzing with frustration.

The first sound he heard on opening the car door was a chainsaw. 'What else?' He grinned and followed the sound across the road to look along the beach.

There Lily was, brandishing the saw, slicing trunks as though they were butter before throwing them out of the way to attack the next section of tree. She looked wonderful. In her element. In control. Being physical. Being useful. Helping the men who were loading a trailer with the results of her efforts.

Max's heart fluttered. He loved her with all his being. This was the woman he wanted to love for ever, to marry, to have a family with. To take chances with and come out the other side stronger and happier than ever. 'I love you, Lily Scott.'

Back at the car, he replaced his shoes with work boots and tossed his jacket onto the seat before striding along to help out, receiving a surprised but heart-warming smile from Lily as he reached for the first log.

After nearly an hour Lily stopped the saw for the final time. 'Job done.' She high fived the other men, and finally him.

'Thanks for that, Lily,' George said. 'I reckon

we've all got enough firewood to last next winter as well.'

'How've you been?' Archie asked Max.

'I'm good. How's Enid getting on?'

'She's fighting. The progress is slow but she's started heading in the right direction. Still be some time before she comes home, though.'

'Glad to hear things are working out.'

Lily stood beside him. 'You coming to my place?'

It was why he was there. 'Yes.' He picked up the chainsaw in one hand and took her hand in the other. 'I have something to tell you.'

Her eyes widened. 'Something good, I hope.'

'Yes.'

Nothing more was said until they'd removed boots, washed hands and walked into the kitchen–cum–family room and stood by the warm fire box.

'Coffee?' Lily asked.

Coffee took time to make. He couldn't wait another minute. 'I've been an idiot, Lily.'

One eyebrow rose and she laughed sadly. 'You're telling me?'

'I love you.'

The laughter died, the eyebrow returned to its usual place. Questions filled her eyes. She stared at him, not moving closer or further away.

Not the response he'd hoped for. His blood

flow slowed. His heart was heavy. Dread crept in where there'd been happiness. He'd told the truth. He needed her to know that. He wouldn't repeat himself. That would sound pathetic. He waited.

'I love you, too, Max,' she said quietly, softly, her voice filled with longing. 'Right from the day we saw each other again after those long years. I wasn't certain, but it felt like love. Love so different from what I've known before. Love for you. It came as a shock to find I might've always felt something for you and had been denying it all along.'

He reached for her and bent close. 'You talk too much.' His mouth took hers, and he kissed her, deeply and filled with what was in his heart. With what he couldn't put into words.

And she kissed him back with what she had managed to say. Love. Her arms wound around him, holding him tight against her.

He melted into her. His love. The one woman who'd got to him, who'd shown him he didn't have to be alone. He did believe in a future with her. Pulling back just enough to look into her eyes, he asked, 'Will you marry me?'

Her smile lit up her eyes. 'Yes.'

His heart picked up its pace. 'Will we raise babies together?'

'Yes.'

'Be together for ever?' He could believe in for ever if Lily was at his side.

'Absolutely.' She stretched up and returned to kissing him.

Kissing wasn't enough. By a long way. Sweeping Lily up into his arms, he headed down the hall to make love. Make love, not have sex. A permanent relationship, not a fling. He'd found his love, his future, his happiness. Now all he had to do was make sure Lily never tired of him, starting by showing her how important she was. 'I love you, Lily Scott. So much my heart is singing.'

'That the noise I can hear?' She smiled up at him, her hand on his cheek. 'I've been wanting to tell you how much I love you and now, well, now you know. This is perfect.'

And it was. Max only got out of bed during the next couple of hours to get a bottle of champagne to celebrate. 'To us.'

'To us.' Lily tapped her glass against his. 'To for ever.'

EPILOGUE

Six months later

TEARS POURED DOWN Lily's cheeks. To heck with the make-up. The look of amazement and wonder on Max's face scrunched her stomach, tore at her heart and lifted her mouth into the biggest smile. 'We've done it,' she whispered. 'We're having a daughter in June.'

Max's cheeks were equally wet as he gazed down at the slight bump at the front of her gown. 'We have, Lily, darling, we have.' He was squeezing her hand, and smiling as if he'd got everything he wanted in life.

They had. Together. As warmth from the sun touched her shoulders, Lily looked up at the blue expanse high above, dotted with gulls dive-bombing the sea beyond her family beach house. 'A perfect day.'

'Not a chainsaw to be heard.' Max leaned in and kissed her cheek. 'You look beautiful.'

Brushing a hand down the front of her cream wedding dress with the full skirt and fitted bodice that accentuated her breasts, she smiled. She had to be the luckiest woman in the world.

'Shall we do this?' Charlotte appeared before them.

'Absolutely,' Lily and Max said in unison, then laughed.

Charlotte had a license to be a marriage celebrant as well as her other qualifications. Now she held up an empty wine glass and tapped it with a silver rod. 'Listen up, everyone. We're about to get underway with the reason you're all here.' She paused to allow everyone to quieten.

Lily looked around at the rows of white fabric-covered chairs with peonies tied to the corners, and felt her heart swelling. Her family and Max's, including his father, just about everyone from the medical hub, friends, and of course Josie and Ollie were here to share their special day. Logan and Michelle stood holding hands at the edge of the group. There was something about the air in Whangaparaoa— romance seemed to take over, putting people together.

Another tapping of silver on glass, and Lily's breasts rose on an intake of that magical air.

Charlotte grinned at her. 'Let's do it.' She

handed Lily the sheet of paper with her vows, but Lily knew them by heart.

'Max.' She reached for his free hand. 'We didn't make it easy for ourselves, but it has been a journey I'll never forget or regret. Along the way I saw your strength, care and kindness, your big heart and most of all your love. I have found my soul mate. I love you with all my heart. Thank you for what you've given me.' She stretched up and kissed him, a salty kiss that was gentle and full of all she had to give him.

'Thanks, sweetheart,' he whispered against her lips, before straightening up and taking his vows from Charlotte. 'Lily Scott, I love you. You've turned my life around, and for that I give you everything. I can't promise to be perfect, but I'll do my best, and I will always love you. And our daughter, and any brothers or sisters she may have in the future.' He got down on one knee. 'Thank you for accepting me into your life.'

Bending down, she kissed him again, then held his hand as he stood up.

Charlotte was wiping a hand across her eyes. 'That's enough.'

Behind them everyone laughed.

'Now you can swap wedding rings.'

Max dug into his pocket and withdrew a box from which he withdrew a gold band. 'Lily, with this ring I pledge to love and cherish you, to care for and protect you for ever as my wife.' The ring slid onto her finger without a hitch.

She stared at it. It felt so right. Perfect. Charlotte was handing her a similar box. Taking out the ring, she reached for Max's hand. 'Max, I pledge to honour and care for you for ever.' She locked her eyes on his, and saw he knew she meant for ever, no getting sick. 'I love you, as my friend, my lover, my fiancé and about-to-be husband.' She had to push the ring hard to get it over his knuckle.

Charlotte grinned. 'I am so happy to say this. I now declare Lily and Max husband and wife. I give you Mr and Mrs Bryant.'

Loud cheers burst out and they were surrounded by everyone, hugging and rejoicing. Until Josie interrupted with a loud call. 'Uncle Max.'

Lily laughed. 'Uncle Max.'

Josie had abandoned her wheelchair for crutches today. She came up to stand in front of her new uncle. 'Welcome to the family.'

Just as Max started to smile, she added, 'Auntie Lily is special. Don't ever hurt her or there'll be trouble from me.'

Max gaped, then roared with laughter. 'I wouldn't dare.' He pulled her into a long hug as all around them laughter filled the air.

Locking his eyes on Lily, he smiled. 'We've done it. I love you.'

* * * * *

If you enjoyed this story, check out these other great reads from Sue MacKay

The Nurse's Secret
Reclaiming Her Army Doc Husband
A Fling to Steal Her Heart
The Nurse's Twin Surprise

All available now!